TAKE ME IN THE NIGHT

TAKE ME #1

R.L. KENDERSON

Take Me in the Night

ISBN-13: 978-1-950918-18-8

Editor: Jovana Shirley, Unforeseen Editing, www.unforeseenediting.com
Cover Designer: R.L. Kenderson, www.rlcoverdesigns.com

NOTE TO READERS

This book is an erotic romance for entertainment purposes only. This story is pure fantasy. Please always practice safe sex and use protection.

Also, the facts surrounding Maddox's case and career might not happen in the real world. We took certain liberties in order to give you the best story possible.

PROLOGUE

ADDISON

TWELVE YEARS AGO

"Shh," Maddox said with a grin as he covered my laughing mouth. "Your father is going to hear." He pulled me halfway across his body as we lay on my bed.

I slipped my hands underneath his T-shirt. "Who cares? Soon, we'll be out of here, and he can kiss my ass."

My father didn't like Maddox. He didn't think Maddox was the *right kind of boy for me*.

What my father meant was that Maddox didn't come from the correct side of town. I was waiting for the day when my father came right out and said that Maddox wasn't good enough for me, but I thought even he knew that would be going too far.

Maddox kissed me. "Addy, we still have two months left. I really don't want anything to ruin our plans now."

"You're right. We've made it the last two years, so we can make it the next two months."

In two months, the two of us would be going to college. Him to the state school and me to the private school. They were only twenty minutes away from each other. Maddox was going to be a doctor, and I was probably going to major in business. He was going to school on a football scholarship, and I was going to school on my father's dime. It made no difference to me as long as the two of us got out of there.

I grinned.

"What's so funny?"

"Two years, two months...the two of us. Everything's in twos," I explained.

His green eyes bright with the plans of our future, he kissed me again. Oh, how I loved this boy. This man. He'd turned eighteen five months ago.

He broke our kiss, and I ran my fingers through his chin-length dark blond hair. He was always saying he should cut it, so my father would respect him more, but I wouldn't let him. I loved Maddox's long hair, and there was nothing he could do to earn my father's respect anyway. Maddox was a Wolfe. He had been born with that stain on his soul, as far as Brantley Graham was concerned.

Maddox glanced at my alarm clock. "I gotta go. I'm supposed to pick up Foster."

I sighed my disappointment. How my father felt about Maddox was how I felt about his brother, Foster. One year younger and on the opposite end of the spectrum from Maddox. Foster already had a juvenile rap sheet as long as my leg, and it was a surprise he hadn't been kicked out of school for skipping so many classes.

He was another reason I couldn't wait to leave our godforsaken small town. I didn't want Foster to take Maddox down with him.

Two months, two months, I chanted in my head.

I gave Maddox a peck. "Okay. Just be careful."

He rolled away from me and shook his head as if he thought I was crazy. "Always, Addy. Always."

I scooted to the edge of my bed and followed Maddox to my window.

He flung one leg over the sill. "I'll see you tomorrow."

I smiled at him. "Promise?"

He grabbed my nightgown and yanked me toward him.

I had to put my hand over my mouth to stifle my laughter again.

"Promise," he said to me. "I didn't get to spend nearly enough time with you tonight."

I longed for the time when we didn't have to make love quickly in case my father came up the stairs or someone caught us in the backseat of his car. "Someday, we'll get to take our time," I told him.

He grinned. "Two months."

I kissed him. "Two months."

He let go of my pajamas. "I'll see you tomorrow."

"Tomorrow," I agreed. "I love you."

"I love you, too." He swiped his finger over my nose and was gone.

I wouldn't see him again for twelve years.

1

ADDISON

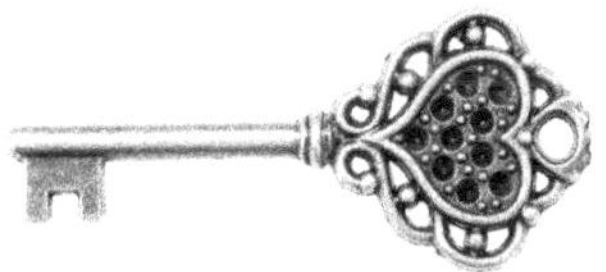

THE PRESENT

"Serena, do you have the Warner file?" I called through my open office door.

I had an intercom, but when it was just the two of us, we weren't very formal. Hell, we weren't very professional, even when we had clients. That was the beauty of living in a small town like Brook Creek. I knew almost everyone, at least by name, and I was the only lawyer within miles who took on the number of pro bono cases I did and charged such cheap fees for the others. They could either take me or leave me.

Serena came rushing into my office with a folder in her hand. "Here you go."

I took it from her. "Thank you. I thought I had lost it."

"At least it's just a will."

I looked at my assistant like she was crazy. "This isn't just any will, Serena. I had to sit with the Warners for six hours. *Six hours*. They own a house and a car and have one child. It should never have taken me that long. That's six hours of my life I can never get back." I shook my head. "I refuse to do that again."

Serena put her fingers to her mouth and giggled.

"It's okay. Go ahead and laugh. I would, too, if I were you. Count yourself lucky that you'd taken the day off."

Her eyes lit up. "Speaking of days off—"

"Serena, what have I told you about taking days off? You just can't," I teased her but pretended to be serious. "I need you way too much."

She gave me a look. "You survived for years without me."

"That's because I didn't know someone like you existed. My last assistant was worse than Karen Walker."

"Who?"

I waved her question away. "Never mind. It was a TV show that was on when I was in high school." I used to watch it with Serena's uncle when my father was out for the night. Well, half-watch it anyway.

"Oh, I know. It's from *Will & Grace*."

I whipped my head up in surprise. "You know *Will & Grace*?"

"Yeah, it's on TV again. It's funny."

"Huh." I remembered hearing something about it coming back, but these days, I rarely had time for TV. "Anyway, you are a godsend. I'm just happy to have you working here."

Serena had just been a girl when Maddox was arrested and taken away. Her mother was Maddox's older sister, who had already started following in their mother's footsteps. Maddox's mom had had Serena's mom, Kelly, when she was seventeen, and Kelly had had Serena when she was sixteen.

Despite Kelly being the oldest, Maddox had been the one to run the family. His mother was too busy drinking and chasing after guys. And Maddox had been the closest thing that Serena had to a dad.

I had loved Serena like a little sister and done my best to stay in touch with her. Despite her family's reputation and limited resources, Serena had graduated with straight As. It wasn't enough to get her a full ride anywhere, but it was enough to get her some scholarships. She was going to take community college classes starting in the fall while she worked with me to help out her family. I couldn't lie that I was relieved that I wouldn't be losing her. And she'd be able to put in more hours with me while she was in college than she'd been able to do while working after school for me.

"And I'm happy to be working here. But…"

"But?" I waited for her to finish before I remembered what we'd been talking about. "Oh, yeah. A day off." I pulled up my calendar on my computer. "When were you thinking?"

Please don't say the tenth. I had a full schedule that day.

"Tomorrow afternoon."

My shoulders sagged with relief. "That's it?"

Serena laughed. "Yes. It's the street dance this weekend." She did a little dance. "It's Creek Days, and I get to go and help my friend set up for the parade on Saturday."

I groaned. Another joy of living in a small town. The annual parade and street dance. I didn't mind the parade, but the street dance was the worst. It was loud and went on until sunrise the next morning. Officially, it shut down when the state said it could no longer serve alcohol, but that didn't stop everyone from going home and drinking till the sun came up.

That also meant that I was usually called down to the sheriff's station at least once in the middle of the night to bail someone out of the drunk tank. It was the downside of being the only lawyer in town.

Last year, I'd had to help get out the Richardson brothers before their mom found out and beat their asses. All because they'd decided to go cow tipping. And they'd had to pick Old Man Flanders. The meanest and grumpiest person in town.

"So, what do you say?" Serena asked.

I'd almost forgotten she'd asked for the afternoon off. "What's on the schedule?"

"Nothing. I think everyone else is too busy to come in."

"Go ahead. I think I'll take the afternoon off, too. Maybe get in some rest before all the chaos starts."

Because, even though the street dance wasn't until Saturday, residents, old and current, would go out to party on Friday, too.

Since my office was downtown and my apartment was above my office, I wouldn't be getting much sleep on Friday or Saturday night. It was still worth it, not to live with my father though.

He was close enough, living up on the hill in the house I'd grown up in. I hadn't quite managed to move away permanently after I lost Maddox, but at least I didn't have to live with my father anymore.

Too bad he still held the reins to my trust fund—aka the money I used to help run my business. After Maddox's arrest, I never wanted someone who needed help to be unable to defend themselves in court. Since there were only about three families in town who had a lot of money, it meant a lot of handouts and cheap billing. But I didn't mind. I'd found my calling, and I loved helping those I could.

If only I could've helped Maddox.

Unfortunately, there was no record of him in the system,

and his case was sealed. It was like he'd fallen off the face of the earth. Not even good old Google could give me anything.

Serena and I went back to work, and at five o'clock, Foster Wolfe walked in to pick up his niece.

Foster nodded hello to me, and I nodded back. He and I were civil toward one another, but I still blamed him for Maddox's incarceration. The two of us didn't talk more than we had to.

The only good thing that had come out of it was that Foster cleaned up his act. He'd gone to school to be a mechanic since he always liked working with cars, and he owned the garage in town. The Wolfe name wasn't such a terrible thing anymore around here—as long as Maddox didn't come before it. People still hated him for what had happened twelve years ago, and no one felt sorry for him in the least. But that was because everyone thought he'd been the one to commit the crime. Only Foster and I knew the truth. Foster because he'd done it and me because Maddox had been with me at the time. I didn't understand why he'd never told anyone that he had been with me that night. I would have vouched for him in a heartbeat.

Part of me hated Maddox for taking the fall for his brother, but I also couldn't fault him completely for looking after his younger sibling. It still didn't mean he'd had to go to prison for the guy though.

I said good-bye to Serena and finished up on the account I had been working on—at least for the day.

It was going to be another night alone for me, so I wasn't in any rush. I didn't know if it was all the thoughts about Maddox or what, but the thought of going upstairs alone seemed worse than usual. I might as well make up for taking tomorrow afternoon off instead.

2

MADDOX

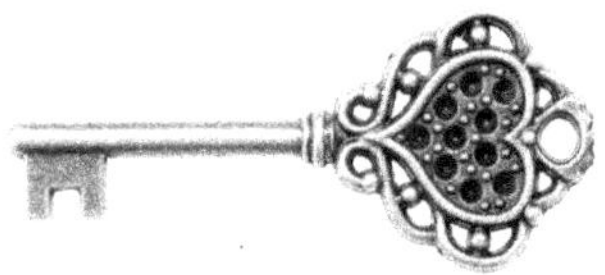

A big, meaty hand slammed down on my shoulder. "We're going to miss you, Mad Dog," my friend and teammate said.

"Yeah, but you'll enjoy breaking in the new kid," I told Flash.

Flash thought he'd earned his nickname because of how quick he was for someone of his size—he was six-three and two hundred thirty pounds of muscle—but it was really because of how fast women scattered when he was around. He was kind of like a big teddy bear, and most females didn't know what to do with him. He might not have been a ladies' man, but Senior Chief Thomas "Flash" Morelli was one of the best damn SEALs I had ever had the pleasure to work with.

He rubbed his hands together. "Fuck yeah, I will. He won't know what hit him."

I laughed, feeling pity for whoever replaced me.

But everybody had to be the newbie at some point.

I still remembered my first day in the Navy like it was yesterday.

I'd been a scared kid, forced far away from the only home I'd ever known, moving to a completely different world from the one I had grown up in. Until then, I'd never even left the state of Iowa. There had been no family trips for me, growing up.

When I'd been arrested, I'd thought for sure I'd be in that jail cell a few hours at most. I knew the security tape pointed to me because Foster had stolen my letterman jacket and put on my baseball cap and a bandana. We looked very different, and I was broader and taller than my brother, but since my brother had kept his face hidden, the sheriff thought it was me. Or maybe he had just wanted it to be me.

Brantley Graham had the sheriff and the district attorney in his pocket and was always looking for ways to get me arrested. I'd kept my nose clean my entire life, only to go down for something I didn't do. But I took the fall because I didn't want Foster to go to prison. Not only had he robbed a gas station, but also a well-known member of the community had died during the commission of the crime, adding on another charge. But I wasn't worried because I was innocent, and I had an alibi.

An alibi who never showed up. An alibi who never vouched for me. An alibi who thought she'd let me rot in prison the last twelve years.

My only saving grace was the judge on my case. I had a bench trial instead of a jury trial, and he pulled me aside and talked to me. Something virtually unheard of. He pulled up the surveillance video, looked at me point blank, and dared me to tell him that it was me in the video.

After being railroaded by the sheriff and the DA, I almost cried that someone finally saw the truth and was on my side.

The judge was no dummy. When he asked me if I knew who had done it, I lied, saying I didn't know, and I thought he knew I'd been untruthful. I didn't know if it was because of that or because of some other reason, but the judge gave me two options: go to prison for twenty years or get the hell out of Brook Creek.

I chose to get the hell out of Brook Creek.

The other stipulation was, I had to leave everyone behind. I thought the judge had been afraid that my old life would drag me back in. It was true that he really couldn't force me to move away in exchange for my freedom, but the only person I cared about had chosen her father's money over me anyway.

The judge dismissed my case with prejudice, and he sealed both my record and the court case. He promised me he was going to look into the sheriff and DA, but he died in a car accident less than six months later. Coincidence? I'd never know.

As a kid with no money, a scholarship that had been yanked the moment I was arrested, and only a high school diploma, I joined the military. After my first four years in the Navy, I told my brother where I really was. I knew Foster was beating himself up for what had happened to me, and I wanted him to know the truth. Turned out, my arrest had helped my brother get his own life on the right track.

I'd helped him buy the mechanic shop in Brook Creek, and he was the one I sent money to every month. He never told my mom or my sisters where it had come from, not that my mom would care too much. As long as she had money for her next bottle of vodka, she didn't ask questions.

Of course, that was why she had cirrhosis now. That, and emphysema from smoking a pack of cigarettes a day.

That was why I had decided it was time to go home.

Even though my mother was a drunk, she was still my mother. And, even though it hadn't been the full twenty years of my theoretical sentence, I was leaving Virginia. My family needed me.

Another one of my teammates walked over to where Flash and I stood. "You have quite the going-away party, Mad Dog," Evan "Ice" Malone told me, his voice laced with sarcasm.

When I'd enlisted in the Navy, there had been rumors about my arrest, even with the records sealed. I had to prove myself to my superiors and to my teammates that I was trustworthy, that I would and could follow orders, and that they could trust me with a weapon. It took time, but it was worth it. I had made my way up the ranks to Chief Petty Officer, and I had the best damn career and military family. It was going to be tough to leave them.

"I didn't want a big party," I told Evan.

It made going back to Iowa even harder. Plus, I had an early flight, and I decided a hangover didn't need to make the trip home with me. I needed my wits to be at full capacity when I got back home.

I was just grateful I wouldn't have to see Addison again. I'd heard how she had gone to college like we'd planned. Part of me was proud of her for getting out, but the other part of me was angry that she'd moved on like I hadn't even existed. I never asked my brother about her, and he never offered up any more information. I supposed I'd run into her sooner or later. Her father still lived in our town, and she was bound to visit him sometime.

"What does Stephanie think about you leaving?" Evan asked me.

I shrugged. "I haven't told her."

Flash spit out the beer he'd just taken a sip of. "You haven't told your girlfriend that you quit the Teams and are moving halfway across the country?"

I took a long drink of my own beer. "Nope. She ghosted me after I told her I was retiring from the SEAL Teams."

"I knew that bitch was a Frog Hog."

I scowled at Evan. We'd broken up, but I'd still dated the woman.

"What? You know that's all she wanted. Status."

Evan was right, but I didn't like to admit he was right.

"Yeah," I reluctantly agreed.

"So, do you care if I call her up?"

"You just called her a bitch," I pointed out.

Evan shrugged. "She's still hot." He grabbed his crotch. "And I have a hog for her."

I rolled my eyes. I should tell him no, but I really didn't care. Stephanie had been fun for a while. I didn't love her, and she didn't love me.

"Go for it."

She'd probably eat Evan alive anyway.

"Is your family excited that you're retired and coming home?"

I took another sip of my beer. "They don't know." Except for my brother.

"What?" Evan asked.

"It's complicated."

Flash was the only one who knew the whole story, and he wasn't talking.

"Is this why you never go home to visit?"

"Pretty much."

"Wow," Evan said. "Everyone's going to be so excited to see you."

Everyone's going to be *something*. I didn't know if *excited* was the right word.

3

ADDISON

Friday afternoon, instead of going home and resting like I'd planned, I was headed to my father's house. I needed to check up on him, and since I'd taken the afternoon off, I decided to get it over with.

When I reached the front door, it opened before I could let myself in or knock.

"Hey, Henry," I said to the butler.

"Miss." Henry nodded and closed the door behind me.

"Do you know where my father is?"

"In the study, miss."

I sighed with frustration and marched toward the study. When I got there, my father was sitting behind his desk.

"What are you doing?" I demanded.

My father jumped in his seat. "I didn't hear you come in."

Once upon a time, my father would have heard me come through the front door. He wasn't the man he used to be. He'd gotten so much older in such a short amount of time. His dark hair was now all gray, and the wrinkles in his face had deepened. His hazel eyes looked tired all the time now. The stroke hadn't helped.

"Daddy, you know you're supposed to be resting. The only reason the doctor let you leave the nursing home was because you'd promised to rest at home."

"But there is so much work to be done."

"Isn't that why you hired Simon? Where is he?"

"He had to go to a meeting since I'm...indisposed."

My father was a proud man and a workaholic. I knew it killed him to be homebound and to only have limited use of his left side. He had to walk with a cane, and he didn't want any business partners to see him looking vulnerable. That was where Simon came in. Simon had become the face of my father's various businesses.

"Maybe you should think about selling some of the properties."

My father looked at me like I was crazy.

He owned the only bank in town and several buildings on that block, including mine. Managing numerous properties was a juggling act that needed constant attention.

"You know what the doctor said about stress."

"This conversation is stressful."

I sighed. He was impossible.

The click-clacks of dress shoes got louder outside the study door, announcing Simon's arrival.

My father visibly brightened upon seeing his protégé. "Simon, how did it go?"

"Very well, sir." Simon looked at me. "Good afternoon, Addison."

His beady eyes leered at me, and his smile made me want to go and shower. His white-blond hair had enough product in it for all of Brook Creek.

"Simon," I said out of politeness. "I was just telling my father that he needed to rest."

When he didn't say anything, I narrowed my gaze at him.

"Ah, yes, sir. You know what the doctor said."

My father put his hands up in surrender. "Fine. I will go back to my room like an invalid."

Of course, my father would listen to a man he'd known for six months rather than his daughter he'd known for thirty years.

"Daddy, you don't have to lie in bed. You could sit on the couch and read or go to the den and watch some TV."

I got the crazy look again. My father didn't *do* television.

"My room is fine, thank you. Can you call Beatrice?"

"Yes."

Beatrice was my father's nurse, and I was sure whatever my father was paying her wasn't enough. I went over to the intercom and put a broadcast to the whole house, asking her to come to the study. My father often gave her breaks, saying she needed downtime. But it was really my father's way of escaping her watch.

A minute later, Beatrice came in and shook her finger at my father. "Mr. Graham, you snuck away again."

"Help me to my room, Beatrice."

"Yes, sir."

Once my father was safely out of hearing distance, I turned to Simon. "You're supposed to be helping him slow down."

Simon put his hands in the pockets of his suit. "I don't work for you. I work for him."

"Yeah, well, if you don't help him slow down, you won't be working for anyone."

"You know, if you would marry me, then your father might settle down."

Ugh. I'd rather die alone with a hundred cats.

"We've already discussed this. I'm not marrying you, Simon."

His thin shoulder shrugged. "Suit yourself. I guess I'll keep doing what I was hired to do then."

Simon went and sat behind my father's large desk. I left the house, exhausted.

It was probably time for me to go home and take my nap.

4

MADDOX

My brother met me at the baggage area in the Des Moines International Airport. I almost didn't recognize him. I supposed he felt the same about me. I'd added three inches of height, added fifty pounds of muscle, and lost several inches of hair since I'd left town at eighteen.

Foster looked the same, just older. I guessed a part of me had been looking for the seventeen-year-old boy I'd left behind. Not the twenty-nine-year-old man standing before me.

"Hey," Foster said.

"Hey."

"Are we supposed to hug or some shit?"

I laughed and held out my hand. "How about a handshake?"

My brother grasped my hand and pulled me into his arms. "I missed you, brother."

I put my arms around him. "I missed you, too." Until now, I hadn't realized how much.

"I'm sorry."

I didn't ask him to explain. I knew what he was talking about. "It was probably for the best."

Foster stepped back. "I should never have let you take the fall. It was . . ."

"Stop." I didn't want to rehash the past. There was nothing that could change what had already happened, so there was no reason to go there. "It's okay. Really." If things hadn't happened the way they did, I never would have joined the Navy and become a SEAL. I would never regret that.

My only regret had long brown hair and big brown eyes. And there was nothing I could do about that either.

Foster smiled. "Thank you."

I was pretty sure there were tears in my brother's eyes as he turned away, but I didn't call him out on it. I felt some of my own trying to escape.

Thankfully, the baggage carousel started up, and luggage began dropping out of the ceiling onto it.

While I watched for my bag, I asked my brother, "Did you tell anyone I was coming?"

"Nah. I thought it would be a nice surprise to bring you to dinner."

I looked at my watch. It was after 2100 hours, and Brook Creek was over an hour away.

"You were supposed to be here six hours ago."

"Yeah, sorry about that, man. I tried to find another flight after my layover was delayed."

Foster shrugged. "No big deal. I'll just bring you to breakfast instead."

I arched a brow. "Will Mom even be up then?"

My brother's smile was sad. "Yes. Now that she doesn't drink anymore, she actually gets up before noon."

Too bad her sobriety had come too late.

"Breakfast it is then." I saw my two huge duffel bags come around the corner. "There's my stuff."

I grabbed my luggage, and we headed to my brother's car.

I whistled upon our arrival. "Wow. When the fuck did you get a 1969 Camaro?"

"About five years ago. I restored this baby myself."

I ran my hand over the hood. "Very impressive."

I couldn't tell in the dim light of the parking garage, but I thought my brother blushed.

"Thank you." He held out the keys. "Would you like to drive it?"

"Fuck yeah."

He threw me the keys, and I popped the trunk. I tossed my stuff in the back and got behind the wheel. I caressed it like a man out of prison with his first woman.

"Are you going to screw it or drive it?"

I laughed. "Drive it. I just wanted us to get to know each other first." I put the key in the ignition and turned the engine over. I almost had an orgasm at the sound of the motor. "Oh, baby."

"She's a beaut, huh?"

"Ohhh, yeah." I put her in drive, and off we went.

If this was how my move home was going to start, maybe it wouldn't be so bad.

We were about five miles outside of town, and I was feeling relaxed and less anxious about seeing my family when lights began to flash in the rearview mirror.

What the hell?

I looked down at the speedometer. I was going fifty-eight in a fifty-five. Hardly what one would call speeding.

With a sigh, I pulled over to the side of the road.

Foster looked over his shoulder. "You weren't speeding, were you?"

"Nope."

"Stupid street dance weekend," he said as he opened his glove compartment. "It's probably the car. The highway patrol sees it and thinks we're some young punks who are out, drinking."

I squinted into the mirror. It was hard to see the details on the vehicle that had pulled us over, and I couldn't tell if it was the state patrol or not.

"Here's the information you need."

I looked over at my brother, grabbed the registration out of his hand, and then fished my wallet out of my back pocket.

A tap, tap, tap sounded on my window, and I cranked the old-fashioned handle to lower the glass.

"Good evening—" I began, only to be cut off.

"Well, well, well, who do we have here? Maddox Wolfe, what the fuck are you doing back in my town?"

I looked up into the face of Sheriff Whitlock.

This prick is still around?

I was so fucking screwed.

5

ADDISON

A pounding at my door had me jumping in my seat.

"Crap." I'd spilled my popcorn all over my lap.

I picked up the remote and hit pause.

I'd been trying to relax since I didn't know how busy I was going to be tomorrow night. I'd already heard people down on the streets, yelling and partying, and it was only a little after ten o'clock.

I threw the blanket off my lap and went to my door. I did a quick scan of my T-shirt for any traces of popcorn before I opened the door.

"Foster?"

His appearance at my apartment was a complete surprise.

"I need you to come down to the station."

Oh no. "Is it Serena?"

"No. She's fine." He paused. "At least, I think she is. I haven't seen her since this afternoon." He waved his hands in front of his face, clearly frustrated. "That's not why I'm here. Can you come down?"

My shoulders sagged. It was only Friday. I wasn't

supposed to have to deal with anything tonight. I blew out a breath. A lawyer's work was never done.

"Sure." I looked down at my clothes. Even though I knew the sheriff and all the deputies, I had probably better put something a little more professional on than sweats. "Give me two minutes to change, and then we can go." I opened the door wider. "Do you want to come in?"

He shook his head. "No, I'd better get back there. Just come, please."

I put my hand on his arm. Despite our differences, he was clearly upset.

"I promise I'll be there. Give me seven minutes." Two to change, five to drive.

Foster was still wound tight, but he looked a little relieved at my words. "Thank you." He turned to go. "I'll see you there."

"Okay." I started to close the door and then whipped it back open. "Wait. You never said who I'm representing."

Foster was already on the stairs, and I couldn't even see him, but he shouted something that sounded like, "My brother."

I shook my head and closed the door to change. I guessed I would find out who had been arrested when I got there.

Seven minutes later, I marched into the sheriff's office in black dress pants and a white blouse. I had grabbed pretty much the first thing I could find in my closet.

I headed straight for the front desk where Martha had worked for the last forty years. I usually didn't even have to say why I was there because she knew I was showing up for whatever client was in jail.

Tonight was the same, except the sheriff himself came around the corner.

"Sheriff Whitlock, I heard you are holding my client. I would like to see him right away." I hoped my client was actually a him, or I was going to look foolish.

Sheriff Whitlock crossed his arms over his chest. "Figures you'd be here, representing him." He dropped his arms and shook his head. He turned and waved me forward. "This way. You know the drill."

Even with the sheriff being friends with my father, he never really liked me much. I didn't know if it was because I had dated Maddox or for some other reason, but he was a pompous jerk. I didn't really care as long as he didn't deny my clients their rights to a lawyer.

I walked in the back and saw Foster first.

"Oh, thank God."

"Hey," I said, putting my hand on his arm. "I told you I would come."

Sheriff cleared his throat. "This way, Counselor. Your client is in interrogation one."

I rolled my eyes as I walked past. Whitlock watched too many detective shows. They only had one "interrogation" room, and it was used more to let people cool off or sober up than it was to interrogate anyone.

We didn't have much crime in Brook Creek.

Except for twelve years ago.

The sheriff turned the knob on the door and pushed it open but didn't enter. I stood just outside to give him my usual spiel.

"Thank you. I'll need a moment alone with my client."

Whitlock smirked. "I bet you do."

What is up with him tonight?

He had never been this rude to me.

He leaned closer to me. "Just so you know, we'll be watching through the mirror." He held up his hands before I could say anything. "We won't have the sound on, but we're going to be watching." He pointed two fingers to his eyes and then one finger at me. "Understood?"

"Understood." I gave him a fake smile. "May I see my client now?"

He stepped back and out of the doorway. "After you…Counselor."

I held in my eye roll this time, stepping through the door where I immediately froze.

Standing in the corner was the last person I'd expected to see.

He wore black cargo pants, a gray T-shirt, and big boots that looked too hot and too heavy for summer. He was taller and broader, but I would recognize those green eyes anywhere. His long hair was gone, as was any love that I used to see in his face.

He stepped toward me. "Hello, Addy."

"Hey, Maddox."

6

MADDOX

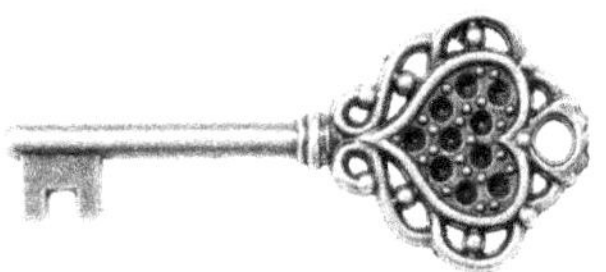

I didn't know who was more surprised—Addison or me.

I certainly hadn't expected her to walk through the door. When Foster had told me that he was going to get a lawyer, I had been so surprised that Brook Creek had one that I didn't even think to ask who the person was.

She turned around. "Please close the door," she said to Whitlock, her voice firm and full of authority.

It wasn't the only firm thing in the room.

Whitlock shot me a dirty look before closing the door, and Addison turned back around.

She gestured toward the table. "Can we please sit?"

I shrugged, pulled out the chair closest to me, and sat.

Addison did the same and took out a notebook and pen from her purse. She started writing things down, and I took the opportunity to study her. Her chestnut hair had been down to her ass in high school, but now, it was only a couple of inches past her shoulders. Her breasts strained against the top, and I was pretty sure they'd gotten bigger since I last saw her, which was saying something because she'd had a pretty impressive set of tits back then.

And I couldn't see it now, but I had noticed her nice, round ass before she sat down. Her black pants were so tight that I was ninety-nine percent positive she was going commando or wearing a thong. No panty lines for Addison.

She looked up at me. "So, can you tell me what's going on?"

"Foster picked me up from the airport. I was driving my brother's car when I got pulled over. Next thing I knew, Whitlock was putting handcuffs on me."

"What for?"

I scowled. "Fuck if I know. That asshole's always had a hard-on for me."

She sighed. "What was his reason? What did he tell you?"

I snorted. "That I was speeding."

"Were you?"

"I was going fifty-eight in a fifty-five."

"Anything else unusual?"

"Other than the fact that I was driving? No."

"As I recall, you didn't always follow traffic laws."

Her comment had me thinking of all the times we'd driven around in my beat-up Chevy truck and the things we'd done in it besides driving. It seemed Addison was thinking the same thing.

I totally recognized the look on her face.

It was the same one she used to give me before she pulled down my pants and sucked my cock into her mouth.

I'd grown up around adults with loose morals, so it was no shock that I'd lost my virginity at fourteen to my mom's friend's daughter. She was sixteen when she came to my house, looking for her mother. Her mom and my mom had left twenty-four hours earlier to go on a bender.

So, Sheila took me to the room I shared with my brother and showed me the things she liked to do in bed. I lasted all of twenty seconds before blowing my load, but thankfully, Sheila gave me a few more rounds that I used to make it up to her.

That was just the beginning. For a while, I had fucked anything that I could.

But Addison had grown up completely different from me. She had been a virgin when she and I started dating. Everything she knew in the bedroom, she'd learned from me. Including how to give the best fucking blow jobs.

I tilted my head to the side. I wondered if she still gave good head.

My eighteen-year-old self demanded I find out. My thirty-year-old self didn't need the complications of being inside Addison Graham again.

"Yeah, well, I've changed along with my driving habits. I was going the speed limit. He had no reason to pull me over."

She wrote the information down and stood. I stared at her ass as she pounded on the door.

"Sheriff, come in here, please."

The door opened thirty seconds later.

"What do you need, Counselor?"

"My client said he was doing fifty-eight in a fifty-five. Give him his speeding ticket, so he can leave."

"Whoa, whoa, whoa. I don't know if he's been drinking."

"Did you give him a Breathalyzer? A sobriety test? Did he smell like alcohol?"

Whitlock gritted his teeth. "No."

"Is he under arrest?"

Whitlock looked pissed. "No."

I shoved my chair back and stood as Addison said, "Then, he's free to leave."

Whitlock stepped around Addison and marched up to my face. "I am going to break you. You're not going to get away with anything like you did twelve years ago."

He was so close; I could smell the stale coffee on his breath despite our six-inch height difference.

I just crossed my arms over my chest and tried not to look bored. This man had no idea the things I'd gone through to be a SEAL. There was nothing he could do to hurt me. I'd already lost everything once, and that was the biggest blow I'd ever taken.

"I didn't get away with anything," I told him.

Movement out of the corner of my vision caught my eye, and I looked over at Addison. She clearly looked confused.

I looked back at Whitlock, who was staring at me, steam practically coming out of his ears. I smacked the top of his arm like we were old friends because I knew it would piss him off, and I walked around him. "Later, Whitlock. Call me when you're ready to break me. You know where to find me."

I walked past Addison and nodded my thanks. I found Foster waiting for me outside the sheriff's office, pacing with panic all over his face.

His look turned to relief when he saw me. "Oh, thank God."

"You can thank Addison."

I heard the sound of her heels coming up behind me.

"I didn't really do anything," she said as she came to stand beside me. "He was just trying to intimidate Maddox, I think."

Foster burst out laughing. "What a putz. My brother is a Navy SEAL and has been to countries like Afghanistan and Iraq. He is not scared of Sheriff Whitlock."

Addison whipped her head and looked at me. "You're a SEAL?"

"Yep." There was no point in denying it.

She turned her whole body toward me. "What did Whitlock mean by, 'You're not going to get away with anything like you did twelve years ago'? Have you been in the Navy this whole time? Did you even go to prison?"

I just raised an eyebrow at her. She didn't need me to confirm the answer she already knew.

She looked at Foster. "How long have you known this?"

7

ADDISON

The next morning, I was still pissed. Everything I'd come to believe over the last twelve years was a lie. My relationship with Maddox, our past, my career. I had decided to be a lawyer to help people like Maddox. Turned out, he hadn't needed my help after all.

I frantically scrubbed a two-year-old stain on my kitchen counter as if today were going to be the day it came off. I was just so pissed.

It sure made sense why I hadn't been able to find any record of Maddox in any prison anywhere in the United States. Or why his case was completely sealed. And I sure as hell had never thought to check military records.

What I didn't understand was why he'd never contacted me, not once, in the last twelve years.

I had cried myself to sleep for months, and he had left without even a good-bye or the thought to contact me all these years. I was on social media. I wasn't hard to find.

I threw the sponge in the sink, wishing it were directed at his face instead.

Plus, it seemed like Foster had known where his brother was the whole time. All those guilty looks weren't for sending Maddox to prison. It was because he had known where Maddox was and didn't tell me.

And, to think, there was a minute last night as I'd watched how cool and calm Maddox was with the sheriff that I actually wondered what it would be like for us to get back together. It was only a moment, but I'd remembered what it was like, being with him. Even though he'd been an eighteen-year-old high schooler, not one of the guys I'd dated since compared to Maddox in the bedroom.

That only pissed me off more.

I looked around for something to do, but I'd already cleaned everything. I needed to get out of there, or I was going to go crazy, cooped up in my apartment.

I changed my clothes, so I didn't smell like cleaning supplies and chemicals. I put on workout gear and left my apartment. I only had to walk six buildings down before I reached my destination. I pounded on the back door, knowing I had to make some noise in order to wake the person on the other side.

Several pounds and minutes later, the door creaked open, and a dark mess of bedhead opened the door.

"Addison, what the hell? It's barely seven on a Saturday morning."

Pete was six years older than me, so we hadn't been in high school together, but we were friends now. He owned the martial arts studio in town, and I had taken a self-defense class from him a few years back. He'd let me use his studio and listened to me vent my frustrations.

"I'm sorry. I just really need to kick someone's ass right now. I was hoping you'd be willing?"

His blue eyes changed to understanding, and he opened the door and let me in. "What's gotten you so riled up that you came here so early in the morning on the weekend?"

"Maddox is back in town."

"Give me a minute. I just need to get changed."

An hour later, after getting my ass handed to me, I said goodbye to Pete. I was feeling much better. I'd done a few rounds on the punching bag while picturing the Wolfe brothers' faces and felt some satisfaction at the thought of hitting them in real life.

My stomach growled, and I remembered I'd been too mad to eat breakfast. The diner was across the street. I figured I deserved a nice breakfast that I didn't have to make myself, so I headed over there.

I opened the door, the bell jingling, when I heard someone yell behind me. I looked over my shoulder to see it was Melanie Kowalski yelling at her youngest to slow down. I turned back to go inside the café and ran into a big, hard wall.

"Ooph."

A warm hand wrapped around my upper arm to steady me.

I looked up into Maddox's green eyes.

"You okay?"

"Yes."

He nodded. "Good." He stepped around me and walked away without a second glance.

I understood why I was upset with him, but there was no

reason for him to be upset with me. I wasn't the one who'd left him.

I watched as he went to the corner, looked both ways, and crossed the street. In one hand was a full bag of takeout containers, and I wondered whom he was bringing food to.

Then, I told myself not to bother. He'd left me. I'd survived the last twelve years without him. I could survive the next twelve. *Good riddance.*

There was a pinch in my chest, and I rubbed my breastbone.

Fuck this.

I was getting upset again, workout for naught. I needed to let it go.

I went into the air-conditioned building and let the cold air wash over me, cooling my thoughts along with my body.

"Good morning, Addison," Ellis Mentz, owner, manager, and full-time employee, called out.

"Good morning," I said as I took a seat at the counter.

She handed a menu to me. "Whatcha in the mood for this morning?"

I perused the laminated piece of paper in front of me. "I was thinking an omelet."

Ellis slid an order form toward her and pulled the pen from behind her ear. "What kind?"

"Denver. And coffee, please."

"You got it," she said as she scribbled my order down.

As she turned to hang it up for the cook, Ellis's daughter came from the back. Dani and I had graduated a year apart.

"Hey, Addison."

"Hey, Dani."

When she reached me, she put her forearms on the

counter and leaned in close. "Did you see who was just in here?"

"Who?" I asked, already knowing the answer.

"Maddox Wolfe."

"Oh, yeah, I saw him."

Dani stood, her eyes round. "You did? What was that like?"

"Awkward."

"Oh," she said, obviously let down. "I thought maybe he would have taken you in his arms and kissed you."

Ha!

"That's not going to happen." *Ever.*

Her eyes lit up. "Do you mind if I go for him then? I don't know what he did while he was in prison, but he looks fine as hell."

I lifted the menu in my hands higher and groaned into it.

Trying to forget about Maddox in this town was going to be harder than I'd thought.

8

MADDOX

The screen door to my mother's trailer still sounded the same after all these years, and I made a mental note to get some WD-40.

My mom was sitting at the kitchen table where I'd left her to get breakfast. To say she'd been surprised to see when Foster and I showed up that morning was an understatement. She'd been so happy to see me, I felt guilty for staying away so long.

Now, she was sipping her coffee and staring out the window. A coughing fit hit her, and it hurt to watch her struggle to catch her breath.

She might not have been the best mother in the world, but she was still mine, and I cared about her.

When she saw me, she looked up and smiled. Her skin was yellow, as were her eyes from jaundice, but she looked genuinely happy.

She patted me on the cheek as I unloaded the food onto the table. "I'm so happy you're home, Maddox."

I took her hand in mine and held it to my chest. "Me, too, Mom. Are you hungry?"

"A little, baby."

I grabbed silverware and plates and brought them to the table just as my brother came out from the hall.

We hadn't talked since last night after he brought me back from the station to our mom's. And that had only been a polite thank-you and good-bye.

Foster rubbed his hands together. "Did you get enough for me?"

"Yes," I said as I took my seat.

I helped Mom dish up her food, and that was when I noticed she was wearing a sweater in June. Her trailer only had a box air conditioner, which wasn't even running. Thank God my old room had its own air conditioner. I had saved up my money one year to buy the thing, so I could sleep in peace, and I was lucky it still worked.

But, now, I was already sweating, and it was only the start of the day. "Mom, aren't you hot?"

"No, baby." She smiled. "I'm fine."

My brother's eyes were sad when I looked over at him. "She has fluid buildup in her abdomen from her liver not working right anymore," he explained. "It makes her cold. We have to go and get it drained once a week at the hospital."

"Jesus."

"Maddox Thane, do not take the Lord's name in vain."

My mother had been an alcoholic with loose morals, but she never used the Lord's name in the incorrect way.

"Yes, ma'am," I said with a smile.

"I know you're upset, Maddox, but I make do."

"It's not fair."

She shrugged. "It's my penitence for the way I lived my life. I've accepted it and made peace."

She might have accepted it, but I hadn't. Not yet anyway.

The three of us finished breakfast, and I cleaned up the kitchen. My brother was outside, smoking, and I went to go talk to him.

Our mother had smoked in her home my whole life, but now that she had emphysema and quit, my brother had to go outside.

"Those things will kill ya, ya know."

Foster took in a long drag and exhaled. "Thanks for the PSA. I hadn't been told that yet." He kicked a rock at his feet. "You know, you used to smoke, too."

I snorted. That had been a long time ago. I had stopped when Addison told me she didn't like kissing me after I smoked. I would have done anything for those kisses. And speaking of Addison…

"Why did you call her last night?"

Foster knew exactly whom I was talking about. He shrugged. "She's the only lawyer in town. I wasn't going to let anything happen to you again."

While I appreciated the sentiment, I still didn't like having her involved. I wanted to stay as far away from her as I could.

"Yeah, this time, the worst thing he could have gotten me on was speeding. You didn't have to bring her down to the station."

Foster shrugged again. "Better safe than sorry."

"Just…just don't do it again, okay?"

My brother raised an eyebrow and took a drag off his cigarette.

"Unless they're going to haul me off to jail. But then

maybe try to find someone else first. I don't care if they're from another town. I don't want Addison involved in my business."

Foster held up his hands in surrender. "Fine. But you should know, she's a damn good lawyer."

"Yeah, well, I don't need her."

"Understood. What are you going to do today?"

"Look for a place to live."

"You don't want to stay with Mom?" Foster asked with a laugh.

"I've been on my own for twelve years, so no. Besides, I don't feel like sweating my balls off every day."

"Yeah, she does keep it warm. I try to visit in the morning or evening, so I don't roast in there."

"She's really sick, isn't she?" I asked. I knew my mother wasn't well, but the reality of her condition was just starting to hit me.

"No, she's not."

"Do you always take her to the hospital?"

"Kelly and I take turns."

"Well, now, you can count me in on the rotation."

"You don't have a car."

I rubbed a hand down my face. "Yeah, that's the other thing on my to-do list today. I might have to borrow one of the loaners from the garage to go looking."

"Fine by me. It'll be nice to have help for Mom's appointments."

I suddenly felt guilty for having been gone so long. I hadn't realized how much my siblings needed me. "Sorry I didn't come home sooner."

"No way," Foster said, shaking his head.

"No way what?"

"You don't get to feel guilty. I'm the reason you went away in the first place. No guilt."

"You know you can't just order someone not to feel guilty."

"Why not? You're a soldier. You're used to taking orders."

"SEAL," I corrected him.

"What?" he said as he threw his cigarette to the ground and used his shoe to put it out.

"I'm—I was a SEAL. Soldiers are Army. I was Navy. I'm a SEAL." I clearly hadn't been around enough if I had to explain this to my brother.

"Well, la-di-da."

"You're an asshole."

"I learned from the best."

"Yeah, well, I don't take orders from you. Besides, I'm your older brother."

Foster grinned. "I can always try."

"Will you give me a ride to the garage?" I said, changing the subject.

"Sure."

"Okay, let me go say good-bye to Mom," I told him. I opened the squeaky door.

"Maddox."

I looked at my brother. "Yeah?"

"I just thought you should know, the building next to Addison's has an apartment open for rent."

I gave my brother the finger and walked into the trailer. My brother's laughter followed me in.

9

ADDISON

I leaned up against the front of my building, off to the side of the big crowd taking up the main drag in town, which had been closed off from traffic. The sun had gone down a while ago, but the streetlights and the lights from the band's trailer on one end of the block put off plenty of light.

I'd said hi to almost everyone I saw and made small talk with a few, but otherwise, I wasn't participating much. I was doing a lot of people-watching as I sipped on my beer. Even though I might have to bail someone out tonight, I wasn't on duty yet.

"Hey, what are you doing over here, alone?"

I looked over to see Pete joining me.

"Not much. Just observing everyone. Wondering if anyone's going to jail tonight."

Pete laughed. "My money is on Jason Mueller."

"Where is he?" I asked as I straightened from my post and got up on my tiptoes.

"Over there." He pointed to the corner where Jason Mueller was stumbling around, clearly drunk.

He yelled at something someone had said and threw his beer can on the ground. It was people like him who'd made glass bottles against the rules at this thing.

"Isn't he too young to drink?" I asked as I dropped down to my heels.

"Nope. He turned twenty-one earlier this year."

"Well, at least he won't get charged with underage drinking." I crossed my fingers he wouldn't be arrested for any other reason, too.

Pete put his hands in his pockets and nodded to the crowd. "How do you feel about that?"

I turned to see whom he was talking about. Despite the event being called a street dance and there being a live band playing, only a few people actually danced. It was more like a street party than anything.

I squinted as I searched the crowd. It took me a second, but once I spotted Maddox, my eyes zeroed in on him. At the moment, he was very close to Dani, who had her hand on his chest and was grinning.

I shrugged. "Eh, I told her she could have him."

Sure, these were the words I'd said, but inside, I was holding myself back from marching over there and punching her in the face.

I had thought about Maddox often over the years, but it seemed I'd forgotten the jealous streak he brought out in me. I had never felt that way about another guy before or since.

That was surely a bad sign.

Maddox looked up from Dani and met my eyes.

"You told Dani she could have him?"

I looked back at Pete. "Yeah. I saw her this morning, and she said something about how fine he was."

"And you're really okay with that?"

Pete had been in college when I dated Maddox, but he knew the same history as the rest of the town. Plus, I'd talked to him a few times about what had happened. He knew how much it had hurt me when Maddox left and didn't contact me.

"Sure," I said. "Maddox and I dated a long time ago. We're ancient history. He doesn't owe me anything, and I don't owe him anything. If he wants to date Dani, he can." Although I couldn't exactly wish them a happily ever after.

"It's best you stay away from him, Addison."

I spun around to see Simon had come up on the other side of me, looking as stuffy as ever. It was a street dance in a small town in the Midwest. He was the only one wearing a suit, and it made him stick out like a sore thumb.

"Your father wouldn't approve."

I chugged the last of my beer, wiped my mouth with the back of my hand, and threw my cup in one of the many trash cans lined up on the street. I crossed my arms over my chest. "What do you want, Simon?"

"You should really act more like a lady. You represent your father."

"No. I represent myself, and I will act any way I please. If anything, you represent my father. That's why you're here, correct?"

Simon pursed his lips.

I smiled. I was right.

"Your father insisted I make an appearance."

I didn't understand why. My father acted like he was the

king of Brook Creek because he had some money when, in reality, nobody cared what he thought.

I never wanted to be like my father.

I waved Simon off. "You made your appearance. You can leave now."

Simon looked at Pete and then took a step closer to me. "Addison, you must consider whom you date. It reflects upon your father."

I pretended to be confused at first. "Oh, you mean, Pete?" I laughed. "You're mistaken. You see, Pete is more likely to date you than he is me."

Pete wasn't gay, but he had an older brother who was, and he knew just what to say to get rid of a closed-minded fool like Simon.

Pete studied Simon. "Nah…he's too skinny. I'd break him in half. He couldn't handle me."

Simon blanched and took a step back. He looked horrified, and I had to pinch the inside of my arm to keep myself from laughing at his reaction.

"You need to consider whom you're friends with, too," he bit out.

"You let me worry about that. Buh-bye now." I turned my back to Simon and faced Pete.

Pete watched him from behind me for a few seconds. "He's gone now."

The two of us burst out laughing.

"That was classic," I told Pete and held up my hand.

He high-fived me. "The look on his face was the best."

After our laughter died down, I told him, "Thank you for your help."

He put his arm around me. "Anytime. That's what friends do."

I stepped out of his embrace after hugging him back. "I think that signals the end of my night."

I took a quick glance toward Maddox again. I could only see his profile now, which probably meant he'd already forgotten all about me. That was my other reason for calling it a night.

I had a comfy bed and a good book that was more fun than watching my ex with a beautiful woman. I was going to have to grow some thicker skin when it came to Maddox and seeing him with other women, but today was not that day. I just wanted to be alone and go to bed.

"See you tomorrow," I said to Pete. "And be good. I don't want to bail you out of jail tonight."

He laughed. "I will. I was just going to talk to Dana Schmidt." He wiggled his eyebrows. "See how she's doing since her divorce."

"You are a bad boy," I told him with a grin.

"Not yet, but I hope to be."

I punched him in the arm. "Good luck. Let me know how it goes."

I said good-bye and walked around to the alley to enter the back of the building and then my apartment. Once I was upstairs, I went straight to the bathroom to get ready for bed. After washing my face and brushing my teeth, I went to the living room and snuck a peek outside.

I knew I should go to my room, but my body didn't agree with my rational reasoning. I looked down at the crowd to where I had last seen Maddox.

He was gone now, and so was Dani.

I scanned the whole crowd. They were nowhere to be seen.

I didn't want to think about what they were doing

together, but now, that was all I would be thinking about. I should have just headed straight to bed.

Calling myself all kinds of a fool, I went to my room, stripped off my clothes, and got in bed. Before I climbed under the single sheet, I checked to make sure my robe was behind my bed in case someone knocked on my door.

It was summer, and I lived in an upstairs apartment in an old building with crappy air-conditioning. The only way to stay cool was to sleep naked with barely any covers and with a fan.

I grabbed my book and tried to shut Maddox from my mind. It took way too long to push him from my thoughts, and it only made me go to bed, feeling confused and crabby. I could only hope sleep would be a little better than reading.

10

MADDOX

I handed Dani my plate that I had practically licked clean. Two minutes ago, it had been filled with blueberry cheesecake. We were in the kitchen of her family's diner. They had closed early tonight and were serving food outside at the street dance instead, so it was just the two of us in there.

"That was the best damn cheesecake I'd ever had."

Her eyes lit up from my praise. "Do you want another piece?"

"No, thank you."

I hadn't eaten a lot of sweets when I was in the Teams, always wanting to keep my body in full physical form, and while I was retired now, it didn't mean I was going to go crazy.

"Well, you know where to come if you ever get a craving," she said and took my plate to the sink.

It was obvious she was talking about more than cheesecake, but I had no desire to go there with her.

When she was done washing both our dishes, I asked her

if she was ready to get back out there. "I'm planning to meet up with my sister and brother."

Dani's face fell. "Oh. I thought maybe we could stay here…and talk."

"Sorry. Maybe some other time."

"Okay," she agreed.

I felt bad for her, but I wasn't going to let her know that. I just played like I didn't know she'd been hitting on me.

Once outside, I told her, "I'll talk to you later. I have to go find Foster and Kelly. Thanks again for the cheesecake."

She looked crushed, and I felt like an asshole, but I wasn't going to fuck her just because I felt bad about hurting her feelings. It wasn't right, especially since it wasn't her I wanted under me.

I found my brother and sister a couple of minutes later.

"Hey, man. How did the car- and home-hunting go?" Foster asked me as he shoved a huge bite of hot dog in his mouth.

"I found a vehicle."

"What'd ya get?"

I hesitated. "A RAV4."

"What the fuck, man? A foreign car? You always go American."

And this was why I'd hesitated.

I shrugged. I'd fallen in love with Toyota while living in Virginia. I just hadn't found the time to break the news to my brother.

"You're a disgrace," Foster said as he shook his head.

I laughed. "Tell me something that I don't already know." I looked over at my sister, who had her arms crossed and was scowling at me. "Still mad at me, huh?"

After my incident with the sheriff, Foster had brought

me home. The two of us had told my mom and Kelly what had happened to me. My mom had just been happy to see me again. Kelly had been pissed. And, apparently, she still was.

Her eyes somehow narrowed even more. "You were gone for twelve years, and you let me think you were in prison."

I shrugged. "I'm sorry. It was better this way."

"I'm your sister."

I put my arm around her. "And I love you."

She pushed me away. "I'm still mad. I haven't forgiven you yet."

Just then, a blur of a person ran toward me and jumped in my arms.

"I'm not mad at you, Uncle Maddox."

I set the young woman down at my feet and put my hands on her shoulders. "Serena?"

She nodded.

"Wow. You've changed so much."

The last time I'd seen my niece was when she was six years old. Now, she was eighteen and looking way too much like a woman.

I looked at my sister. "How do you let her leave the house?"

The corner of my sister's mouth twitched, but she held her frown. "I say a lot of Hail Marys."

"If I were your mom, I'd never let you leave." I gave Serena the side-eye. "Do you have a boyfriend?"

She giggled. "Maybe."

I yanked her into my arms. "I missed you, kid."

Her father hadn't been around from day one, and I had helped my sister out a lot with Serena. I felt like I'd helped raise her in the beginning.

"I missed you, too," she said so softly, I almost didn't hear her over the band and people talking.

As Serena stepped back, I saw one of the two men who'd been talking to Addison earlier. The first guy was Pete. It had been over a decade, but he looked like an older version of himself. And he was currently hanging out with someone who wasn't Addison, so I dismissed him.

But the second guy…there was something about him I didn't like.

I nodded to the man. "Who's that?"

"That's Simon," Serena said.

I was surprised she was the one who'd answered.

"Who's Simon?" I asked.

"He works for Addison's dad. He wants to marry her, but she'd rather remove her eye with a dull spoon."

I raised my eyebrow.

Serena laughed. "That's what she said, not me."

"So, Addison doesn't like him?" I asked.

"Nope. But he doesn't take the hint. She told me he brings up marriage at least once a week."

The Simon guy was puny and looked like a weasel. He was wearing a suit and stood out in the crowd. People were actually laughing at him behind his back.

Yet I couldn't stop the possessive feeling that came over me that this guy was trying to push my Addison into marrying him.

Who does this asshole think he is?

"Uncle Maddox?"

"Hmm?" I said while keeping my eyes on Simon.

"You look like you're going to kill him."

Serena's words broke the spell, and I looked at her. "I'm sorry?"

"You looked like you were going to kill him," she said with her brow raised.

I looked at my brother and sister, who both nodded. My sister rolled her eyes, and my brother was stifling a laugh.

I turned my gaze back to my niece. "I'm sorry if I scared you."

She wrinkled her nose. "You didn't scare me. But, if I were Simon, I'd run far away from here."

"I'm not going to hurt him," I protested.

She held her hands up in surrender.

"Brat," I told her, and she laughed.

It was true. I wasn't going to hurt the Simon character. I had a lot more discipline than that. If I could sit in one spot for thirty-six hours straight while hiding from the enemy in a foreign desert, I could keep myself from punching one guy.

However, a few kind but firm words, warning him to back off, wouldn't kill anyone.

My eyes went from Simon up to Addison's apartment window. It was obviously closed due to the noise from the street dance, but I couldn't help but wonder if she kept her bedroom window unlocked like she had when we were in high school.

I shook my head.

On second thought, it would be wise for me to keep my distance from anyone in Addison's circle. If I were smart, I'd leave her to get rid of Simon on her own.

Too bad I couldn't stay away from her.

11

ADDISON

My eyes popped open, and I sucked in a short breath.

My body was on full alert, but I couldn't figure out what had woken me.

I stared up at my dark ceiling as I slowed my breathing, so I could listen for any noise.

I could hear crickets outside, playing their nightly tune, but that was it. The street dance must have ended some time ago because I didn't hear any music or voices.

I waited a few more seconds and rolled to my side to reach for my phone. Maybe a text message had pulled me from my sleep. I should check to see if it was important, although if it was, I should have gotten a phone call instead.

I put my hand on my nightstand, missing my cell, when I saw movement out of the corner of my eye.

A large, imposing figure rose from the old wicker chair I kept in the corner of my room.

I should've been scared that someone had gotten into my

apartment while I was sleeping, but I knew right away that it was Maddox.

I had no idea how he'd managed to get in, but from the things I'd read about Navy SEALs, they had a way of getting into areas that average humans couldn't.

A wave of excitement flooded my body, starting at my head and my toes, converging to the area between my legs.

He slowly approached the side of my bed. When he reached me, he looked down as if he was studying me.

He hooked one finger under the sheet covering me, keeping his eyes on mine. He slowly pulled the fabric down and off my body. When I heard him suck in his breath as the sight of my nakedness hit him, a rush of satisfaction went through me.

He still found me attractive.

I watched, fascinated with his body, as he pulled off his T-shirt. He had been muscular in high school since he played football, but his muscles now had to be twice as big. His arms were huge, and his stomach sported an eight-pack.

God bless streetlights.

I ran two fingers down his toned abs as he undid his belt and pushed his cargo shorts off his hips.

His big, gorgeous cock sprang out from the confines of his clothes. This time, I was the one who sucked in a breath.

This was the first penis I had ever touched, sucked, and put inside my body. Was it possible that it was bigger than I remembered?

I didn't get to find out because Maddox knocked my hand away as he kicked his shorts off his feet.

He put one knee on the bed and pushed my legs open, exposing me to him.

He pushed two fingers into me and groaned. I knew what he had found. I was wet. I was always wet for him.

I clenched around him, and he rubbed my clit. My back arched slightly off the bed, and my eyes closed of their own accord.

I couldn't believe he still remembered how to touch me, but I really shouldn't have been surprised. Maddox had bedroom skills, even back in high school. I'd been with grown men who had no idea what to do with a vagina.

I forced my eyes open just in time to watch Maddox take his hand from me, and he rubbed it over the head of his dick. He was using my desire as lube, and it was so hot; it only made me wetter. I could feel it coating the inside of my thighs now.

Maddox stood and pulled me to the end of the bed. He ran his hand down my body and then pushed both my knees back to my shoulders. He circled my wrists in his hands, and as he pushed my arms over my head, he shoved his cock inside me.

A hiss sounded from the back of Maddox's throat, and I almost came all over him. He continued to push until he bottomed out, and there was no more room for him inside me. It had been some time since I was with someone of his considerable length, and my body wasn't used to it.

I welcomed the bite of pain though. It brought me back to when he'd taken my virginity. Except, now, I had much more experience.

I rocked my hips up and down over his dick to get it to rub the spot inside me that would complete my orgasm.

Maddox had other ideas.

He dropped all his weight on me, and that extra inch that hadn't fit was now inside me.

I closed my eyes and commanded my body to relax around him. As if he knew what had happened, Maddox didn't push my body any further at that moment.

As I felt my body give and my legs fell more to the side, I opened my eyes and looked at him again.

Maddox stared at me as he slowly pulled his cock from my body and then pushed back in. Thankfully, there was hardly any pain at all.

As if he sensed what was going on inside me, he began to pump his hips, picking up speed, his rhythm on point.

My almost climax was barreling down on me at full speed, and I could tell it was going to be epic. I hadn't had a really good orgasm from anyone other than myself for a long time, and I clenched my eyes shut to keep it at bay. The longer I held it off, the better it would feel.

Maddox's breathing quickened, and I knew he was close, too. I wanted to touch him, to claw at his back for making me feel so good, but he still held my wrists above my head.

Right before I exploded, Maddox bit my neck, and my eyes flew open. He put his nose to mine as I shuddered and convulsed around him. I barely saw the look of satisfaction in his eyes, as my orgasm was so strong, but I did, and ironically, it made me come harder.

Maddox pumped into me a couple of more times and then quickly withdrew from my body. He let go of my arms as he stroked his cock with his hand, coming all over my belly.

He pushed himself back inside me as he rubbed his seed into my skin, as if he was leaving his mark all over me.

I watched him do this, his face so full of concentration that I could only stare. I wanted to be in his head right now. I wanted to know what he was thinking.

Had he come to my room with the intention of fucking me? Why had he come at all?

When he seemed satisfied with his work, he pulled his shaft from my body and stood completely. He looked around until he found his clothes and then proceeded to put them on. I knew he was leaving, and a part of me wondered if he was trying to humiliate me.

If that was what he wanted, it wasn't going to happen.

I lay there, making no move to cover myself or do anything to show him that I regretted what had happened between us.

I was no longer the shy virgin he'd deflowered, and I had been with more men than I could count on both hands.

Plus, I didn't regret what had happened just now. Maybe I would in the morning, but in the dark of the night, with sleep still hanging over me, I was just grateful for the good fucking.

I closed my eyes for a moment. I was relaxed and sated, and I knew sleep would consume me again soon.

I wanted to catch one glimpse of Maddox before he went, but when I opened my eyes, he was gone. He'd left as silently as he'd come.

I moved back to the middle of my bed and pulled up my sheet. As I drifted off, it finally hit me that we hadn't spoken a single word to each other the entire time.

12

MADDOX

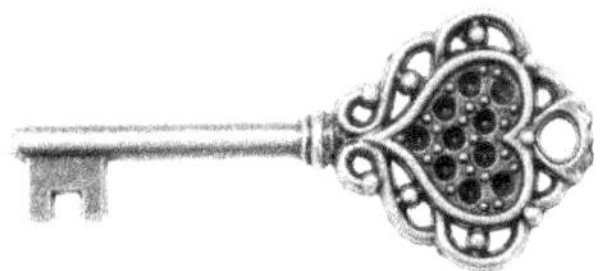

I rested my head against the back of Addison's building. If it hadn't been made of brick, I would have pounded my forehead against it a few times.

What did I just do?

Fucked the shit out of her, my stupid brain answered.

But I already knew that.

What I meant was, what had I done to our relationship? Was she going to think we were some sort of couple now?

She was a firecracker in bed and the best goddamn lay I'd ever had, but she was never going to be more than that. I had learned my lesson already.

Yet, as I stood there, I couldn't forget the way she'd responded to me. She'd been so wet. No one ever got as wet as Addison. One woman I'd dated came close, but she'd always been self-conscious about it, even after I told her it was a good thing.

But Addison hadn't been embarrassed in the least. Not even after we were done fucking, and I was putting on my clothes.

Things had definitely changed. She'd always covered up after we had sex in high school. But not tonight.

I had almost fucked her again just from her display of confidence.

I adjusted my stupid cock in my shorts.

Down, you fucker.

I wasn't going to screw her again.

Except all I could think about was everything I'd missed out on. The taste of her sweet pussy, her tongue on my dick, her breasts, her mouth...I hadn't even kissed her.

It was kind of surprising she hadn't kicked me out of her apartment.

I took a step away from the wall and shook my head.

I needed to stop thinking about having sex with Addison. So I didn't get to experience everything I had years ago. I would get over it. I hadn't slept with her for twelve years. I could certainly go another twelve.

I looked at her bedroom window as I walked away. Course it had been easier when I didn't have to see her tempting body everywhere I went.

If my SEAL teammates could see me now, they'd call me a pussy.

Good thing they aren't going to see me anytime soon, I thought as I walked to my mom's trailer. It was about a mile away, but that was nothing for me. And the night was beautiful. It would give me time to clear my head.

I needed to work on getting a place to live tomorrow. I was thankful I had found my SUV earlier, but it had taken all day. I'd had to travel almost an hour away just to pick it up. It hadn't left any time to look for apartments. I was hoping to be done tomorrow, so I could start working at the garage on Monday.

When I reached my mother's, I tried to be quiet, but the squeak of the door gave me away. My mom was just sitting up on the couch as I walked in. The TV was the only light in the room, but I could tell she'd been sleeping.

"Mom, why don't you go and sleep in your bed?"

She waved away my suggestion. "I'm so used to sleeping on the couch. I can't sleep on my bed anymore."

More like she was used to passing out on the couch, but I wisely kept my mouth shut. I didn't want her to feel bad for her past.

"I'm sorry I woke you."

"It's okay, baby."

"Well, I'm going to head to bed," I said as I started for my old bedroom down the hall. "You should go back to sleep."

I was almost out of her sight when she said, "You need to stay away from her, Maddox."

I stopped. "Stay away from who?"

My mom sighed. "Addison."

My shoulders slumped, and I turned around. "Mom, I don't want to have anything to do with her."

"That's what you say, but I know men. They think with their junk."

"Mom."

"I might have been a drunk, but I'm not a dummy. How do you think you and your brother and sister came about?"

"Because you got involved with losers."

"*Maddox*."

"I'm sorry, Mom." But it was true.

All three of our dads had bolted the second my mom told them she was pregnant. Foster had met his dad once when he was around eleven or twelve, but Kelly and I had only ever seen pictures. The way my brother had sat by the window for a week, waiting for his dad to come back a second time, made me grateful I'd never met my sperm donor.

"I just don't want to see you hurt, baby. The girl left you high and dry when you needed her most."

"Mom."

"Maddox," she said over me, "I know you were with her that night. I know she never told anybody. She was too embarrassed to admit she was with a Wolfe. She left you to rot in prison." She pointed her finger at me. "You stay away from her."

I nodded in agreement. I didn't know if I agreed, but I just wanted to go to bed and not argue.

"Good." She lay back down. "I'll see you in the morning, baby."

"See you in the morning."

I went to my room, and then I shut and locked the door. I stripped off my clothes and flopped backward onto the bed.

My mother's words reverberated in my head. She was right about Addison not being there for me. But I didn't know if she had been embarrassed. We'd had plans after high school. We were going to be together. She'd never made it seem like she was ashamed of me.

I sighed and put my arm behind my head.

Maybe I was letting her off too easy. But, right now, it was hard to be mad at her when I could smell her on my cock. Funny how I'd come all over her, wanting to mark her, and I was the one with her mark on me.

I knew she wasn't innocent though. She had left me high and dry, as my mother had said. She might not have been embarrassed, but she apparently hadn't loved me enough to take on her father's wrath.

I really did need to stay away. I was never going to keep a clear head if I couldn't keep my dick out of her.

I was going to have to find her tomorrow and let her know I was sorry. I should never have snuck into her room, I should never have pulled her covers down, and I should never have had sex with her.

I was sure she would agree that it had been a mistake as well. She hadn't been warm and friendly since I came back to town. I didn't understand why, but she was obviously as upset with me as I was with her.

I didn't know where that was coming from, but it would probably be wise to make sure she didn't press charges.

I rolled over. I needed to get my head on straight.

I wasn't eighteen years old anymore.

I needed to start acting like it.

13

ADDISON

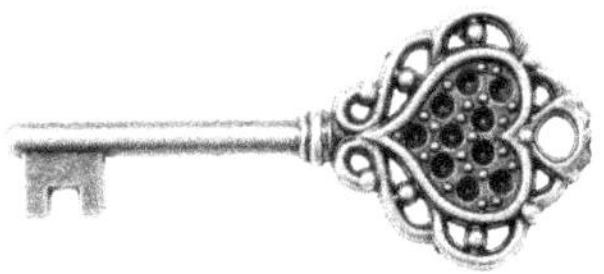

"Addison, stop fidgeting in your seat. It's unladylike."

Easier said than done. My father wasn't the one who'd had a big ole dick inside him last night. I was sore and couldn't get comfortable. I'd picked the wrong underwear to wear. I should have grabbed my big granny panties that I used when I had my period instead of my thong.

I picked at my dinner while I gave him the finger under the table. I had learned years ago to keep my rebellious thoughts to myself. And, even though I was a grown woman now, it wasn't worth starting a fight.

It was my weekly Sunday dinner at my father's house, and tonight, I wanted it to be over more than ever. I yawned for what felt like the thousandth time that night. Despite falling into a post-orgasmic sleep after Maddox had left, I was tired today.

Although that could be due to whoever had woken me up at six in the morning. There had been a loud crash in the alley under my window this morning. When I peeked out the window, I saw a group of guys walking away. I still didn't know what the noise had been or if they had been up early or not even gone to bed last night, but I did know they'd woken me up. And, after that, I couldn't fall back asleep.

I kept replaying sex with Maddox over and over in my head. In the light of day, it almost felt like it hadn't been real. Except for my sore vagina, that was.

While the sex had been phenomenal, I was pissed about the whole thing. He'd barely spoken to me, outside of me being his interim lawyer. No, *I'm sorry for leaving*, or, *I missed you*. Nothing. And then he had come into my home in the middle of the night, and I'd just spread my legs for him.

I was just as mad at myself as I was with him. I hadn't even made him work for it.

"Simon tells me that you have been hanging around Pete Hagen."

I shot Simon a look. *Blabbermouth.*

He sneered at me in return. He knew exactly what he was doing.

"Yes, he's my friend. Are you going to tell me who I can and can't be friends with?"

"Of course not, dear. I just want to make sure that is all you are."

My father was unbelievable.

"Not that it is any of your business, but yes, we are only friends. I'm not dating anyone."

"Good." My father took a bite of food. "Speaking of dating, I know that Maddox Wolfe is back in town." His jaw clenched as if the words were hard for him to say.

"You're correct. I've run into him once or twice."

My father pursed his lips. "Yes, well, Simon and I think it's best that you stay away from the Wolfe boy."

It was unfortunate that I had taken a drink of my wine at

the same time my father said that because I almost spit it across the table. Instead, I tried to swallow it and immediately began coughing as it went down the wrong tube.

The fact that my father had called Maddox a boy was hilarious. There was nothing boyish about him. He was all man.

"Addison, control yourself," my father said.

God, he could be such a dick sometimes.

"I'm sorr-sorry my chok-choking is offensive to y-you."

Not to mention, it was only the three of us. It wasn't like we were in the midst of company.

My father's face softened a little as I grabbed for my water glass. "I apologize. I know you're not doing it on purpose. But perhaps you should excuse yourself to use the bathroom."

Good idea.

I got up, taking my water with me, and went down the hall to the bathroom. After getting my breathing under control, I used the toilet and adjusted my clothing to make myself more comfortable.

After leaving the bathroom, I skipped the dining room and took my glass to the kitchen to drop it off. I said a quick hello to the staff and went to grab my purse. Then, I went back to the dining room to bid my father good-bye.

"Addison, where do you think you're going?"

"I decided you were right, Father. I should excuse myself."

"I didn't mean for the whole night. You haven't finished your dinner."

"Addison, you are being disrespectful to your father," Simon had the audacity to say.

And he wondered why I didn't want to marry him.

"I've had enough to eat, thank you," I said to my dad. "I'm leaving right now out of respect, so I don't say anything I will regret," I told Simon. "Have a good night." I spun on my heel and walked away.

"We're not done discussing the Wolfe boy," my father called out to me.

I put my hand up in the air and waved. The conversation was over as far as I was concerned.

I hurried to my car before my father could send Simon after me. My engine didn't want to turn over right away, and I slightly panicked. On the third try, the car started. As I put it in drive, I made a mental note to take it in to be looked at. I shuddered at the thought of having to spend the night at my father's with him lecturing me all evening.

When I got home, I parked behind my building in one of the two parking spots. Someday, I would have a house with a garage where I wouldn't have to deal with ice and snow in the winter. There was a lot of shade in the back, so summer was always easier even if my vehicle still got hot, and I couldn't pass up being able to walk downstairs to my office every morning.

The building next to me had an unfamiliar SUV parked with the back facing the door. It was wide open, as was the door to the building. It looked like someone was moving in.

The building was owned by a couple of brothers. Scott and Michael Carson were both accountants with their business on the bottom half. They used to live above their office, like me, but then they'd each gotten married—one about two years ago and the other about six months ago—and the place had been vacant since.

Because I had nothing else to do, I figured it would be

nice of me to stop by and say hi. Maybe offer some assistance if need be.

I peeked in the doorway and didn't see anyone.

"Hello?" I called up the stairs.

There was no answer, but I could hear the pounding of what sounded like a hammer, so I decided to just head up to the second floor. The door to the apartment was open, too, so I knocked before stepping inside.

"Hello? I just wanted to welcome you—what the hell?"

There, in all his shirtless, sweaty glory, was Maddox Wolfe. His jeans were resting low on his hips, his V demanding that I lick it.

Of course Maddox was my new neighbor. I should have known.

Maddox turned and let his hammer fall to his side. "Addison."

I crossed my arms over my chest. "What are you doing, Maddox?"

He lifted his hands and rotated his body. "I thought it was obvious. I'm moving in."

"Ha-ha," I said mockingly. "You know what I mean. Why are you moving in next door to me?"

"The rent is cheap, and it was available." He took a step closer to me. "Believe it or not, Addison, not everything is about you."

I flinched. "I never said it was," I said as I raised my chin.

I knew I should turn around and leave. Nothing good would come of me being here, but his comment really pissed me off. I'd been told a time or two that I had a temper.

I wiggled my fingers at him and sneered. "You're welcome to live where you want to, and as long as you keep your dick over here, we should be fine."

Maddox's eyes changed, and I recognized that look. It was full of determination and sex. I instinctively took a step back, but it wasn't toward the door. We must've moved around in the midst of our conversation, and my butt hit the island counter. And, while I could have bolted to the right, I was transfixed. I made no other attempt to move.

14

MADDOX

I took a step toward Addison. "Why are you so dressed up? Hot date?"

"Wouldn't you like to know?"

I lifted a shoulder. "Must not have been that hot if you're home before dark."

She grunted. "I was at my dad's. It's our weekly dinner."

I put my hands on her hips and lifted her onto the counter. "Good."

"What are you doing?" she asked, her brown eyes wide.

Pulling her crotch toward mine, I said, "Keeping my dick over here." I let go of her waist and slid my hands under her skirt, up her thighs, and over her hips. "Bad girl. Do you always go to dinner at your father's without underwear?"

She squirmed against me. "No. I had to take them off. I was a little sore from last night."

Male chauvinist pig alert. I fucking loved that she was sore because of me. It meant that she'd had a reminder of me and my cock all day, and it meant that nobody had stretched her pussy like I had. At least, not for some time.

"I'm sorry I hurt you."

"I'm not."

I raised an eyebrow.

"I mean, don't do it again."

I chuckled and pushed her back onto her elbows. I lifted her knee-length skirt and bared her pussy to me.

"What are you doing?"

"Shh. I'm looking."

She was pink and swollen, and I immediately felt bad.

Poor pussy.

I gently kissed her on her cleft.

I heard her breathing change, and I smiled.

I didn't want to touch her because my hands were dirty, so I put my thumbs on the very outside of her cunt and pulled on the skin. She opened for me like a flower.

A fucking naughty flower that needed to be licked.

Taking her soreness into consideration, I tenderly touched her with my tongue at first.

Addison's head fell back between her shoulders.

I started at the bottom and made my way up to her clit where I paid extra-special attention, circling it until I had her hips moving.

"Oh God." She lifted her head. "I thought you said everything wasn't about me."

"This isn't for you. This is for me."

I sucked one of her feminine lips between my lips. And then the other.

"Did you always taste this good?"

"I don't know. Were you always this good at tasting?"

I grinned against her wetness and turned all my attention to making her come with my mouth alone. I might have taken my time though because, like I'd said, I was doing this for me.

After I felt like I'd teased her enough, I flicked her magic little button with my tongue until she exploded all over my face. So, that still did the trick after all these years. Some things hadn't changed.

I stood up and took my hands from Addison's body even though I wanted to be inside her now.

When I looked up into her eyes, she had the same look she'd had in the jail the other night.

She reached for my fly, and in one swift move, she had it open, the zipper down, and my cock in her hand.

I hissed at the feel of it in her fist.

She rubbed the head of my shaft between her slit.

I shook my head. "You're sore."

She sat up, put her forehead to mine, and nodded. "Go slow. No sudden movements."

I didn't thrust inside her, but I didn't pull away either.

"Please, Maddox." She kissed my jaw. "Please."

"Oh God." I was always such a sucker for her.

I gradually pushed my dick into her body as I put my mouth on her shoulder and sucked.

I heard a slight whimper, and I stilled, but she put her hands on my ass and urged me forward.

This time, I didn't stop until I was all the way inside her. I kept our bodies connected as I rocked our hips against each other's.

It was so different from last night, but it was still just as hot. And, when Addison wrapped her arm around my neck and her whimpers turned to cries, I knew she was going to come again, and I was done for.

The moment I felt her clench around me, I let myself go.

Her mouth moved down to my neck, and she bit down from the force of her climax. It was going to hurt later, but right now, I didn't mind in the least.

I loved how our bodies were connected in two places as I poured my seed inside her.

I lifted my head away from hers. "Are you okay?"

She smiled and nodded. "Yes. You?"

"You're shitting me, right?"

She laughed.

"Maddox," a voice came from down the stairs.

Addison gasped.

It was Foster.

I quickly pulled my cock from her body and zipped up my jeans. I grabbed my hammer and went back to the picture I'd been trying to hang.

"Maddox—oh, Addison, you're here."

I looked over my shoulder to see her still sitting on the counter where I'd left her, but now, her skirt was pulled down, her ankles were crossed, and she was swinging her legs back and forth in a relaxed pose. As if I hadn't just given her a fucking orgasm.

I turned back to my wall and shook my head. She was good.

"Foster," she said in greeting. "I came over to say hi to my new neighbor. Imagine my surprise when I found it was Maddox."

"Uh…yeah," my brother said.

I looked behind me again.

Addison jumped off the counter, and I briefly saw her wince. It was only for a second, and I was pretty sure my brother missed it.

"Well, I'd better get home. Let me know if you need help

with anything, Maddox."

"Will do. Thanks for stopping by."

She walked past my brother, and then she turned and gave me a smile.

And then she was gone.

"What's up?" I asked Foster.

"Were you two fuckin'?"

"What the hell, Foster?"

"Call me crazy, but I swear, I can smell sex in the air," my brother said.

"Oh, Foster," Addison said from the doorway.

Foster jumped a foot in the air and burst out laughing. His face turned red, but he turned to look at Addison. "Yeah?"

"I'm going to bring my car in tomorrow. It's not working right."

My brother swallowed. "Okay. Sure. That should be fine." He held up his hand, obviously flustered. "Can you do Tuesday instead?"

"Yep." She beamed at him and walked away.

My brother breathed a sigh of relief.

"Oh, and, Foster?" Addison called from the stairs.

"Yeah?"

"Yes, we were fucking. Thanks for waiting until we were done."

I'd never seen my brother more embarrassed in his life.

15

ADDISON

On Monday, I went to Des Moines for the day to meet up with some friends. We'd decided to play hooky and go shopping instead. Plus, I needed some girl time.

Pete was kind enough to trade cars with me for the day in case mine broke down. I didn't want to get stuck out of town, and Pete didn't have plans to go anywhere far, which was a relief because I needed to get out of Brook Creek.

Des Moines was the largest city in Iowa, and sometimes, I considered moving there. There was so much to do. You didn't know everyone, and they didn't know you. And there were no ex-boyfriends that haunted my past there. At times, it made me ask myself why I still lived in Brook Creek.

"So, after twelve years of just—*poof*—being gone, Maddox shows up, back in town?" Marie, one of my closest friends, asked me as she rubbed her huge belly.

I was going through a bunch of shirts on a clothing rack while she stood next to me with a look of incredulity on her face.

"That's right," I said as I pulled a cute top off the rack and looked it over.

"And he never went to prison?" my other good friend Darcy asked.

"Nope."

I had already told the ladies about Maddox sudden reappearance. It was one of the reasons I wanted to meet up today with them. It was too important to discuss over the phone, and I needed their advice on how to handle the situation.

"What happened to him then? I mean, how did he end up going into the military?" Darcy asked, taking the shirt from me and holding it up under my chin. She shook her head.

I shrugged and took the shirt to hang back up. "I still don't know. His record is sealed."

"You haven't asked him?" Marie asked.

"Um...I haven't had the opportunity to ask. We've either been not talking to each other or..."

"Fucking like bunnies," Darcy finished for me.

"Yeah, that. Although I wouldn't say we were bunnies," I said with a laugh.

"I can't believe he just came in your room, didn't say a word, and had sex with you," Marie said, her dark eyes wide.

"I think it sounds hot," Darcy countered with an almost-dreamy look in her own blue eyes. "I wish someone would sneak into my room and ravish me."

"Not me. I need to be wooed," Marie said.

"Says the woman with the most romantic husband in the state," Darcy said. "Not all of us are as lucky as you. He probably gives you six orgasms a night and apologizes for not giving you more."

Marie's husband, Desmond, was tall, dark, and handsome, but he was also one of the nicest guys in the world, and he doted on her.

"Yeah, I am lucky, aren't I?" she said with a smile as she hugged her growing belly. Her beautiful dark skin was practically glowing.

"You are lucky," I told her. "Now, feel sorry for the rest of us."

Marie laughed.

I picked up another shirt and held it up to her. "This would look great on you."

She took it from me. "It's adorable. But I should probably wait to buy clothes until after I have this baby." She put the shirt back and looked at her watch. "Is it time for lunch yet?"

"What time is it?"

"Eleven."

"I could eat," I said.

"Sure," Darcy agreed, pushing her blonde hair over her shoulder.

We left the store and walked down the mall to the restaurant we had previously decided on. I put our name in with the hostess, and we waited to be seated.

"So, what are you going to do about Maddox?" Marie asked me.

"I honestly don't know. Part of me is still really angry with him, but then the two times we were together, I really enjoyed it. Not just the sex," I clarified. "I like that I forgot about what had happened. I like that we could just be together."

"But you know that, eventually, your resentment will probably get worse."

I leaned my head back against the wall of the bench we were sitting on. "I know." I lifted my head as a thought occurred to me. "I forgot to tell you ladies. The weird thing is, I feel like Maddox feels the same. From the moment I saw him again, I feel like *he's* the one mad at *me*. But I can't figure out why."

"Addison for three," the hostess called out.

We followed her to our table and took our seats.

"You don't think Maddox blames you for getting sent away, do you?" Marie asked.

"I can't imagine why. I went to the sheriff right away and told him that Maddox was with me at the time of the robbery."

"Yeah, but you never went to court and testified," Darcy pointed out.

"I would have. He's the one who never asked me to go to court for him."

Marie gave me a sad smile. "Maybe it's because he found out he wasn't going to jail. Whatever happened that caused him to go into the military instead of prison, he didn't ask you to testify because he didn't need you anymore."

I flinched at her words.

Marie grabbed my hand. "Oh, hon, you know that's not what I meant."

I squeezed her fingers to let her know I wasn't offended. "I know. But maybe you're right. Maybe he saw his opportunity to escape Brook Creek and his family, and he took it. Maybe I would have weighed him down. Maybe I would have been a reminder."

"It still doesn't make it right that he just ditched you." Darcy said.

"I know."

But I had to wonder, *Would I have done the same thing if I were him?*

And then I remembered all the nights I had cried for him. No, no way. I would have tried to take him with me. I would have at least said good-bye.

"Now, you know why I don't know what to do with him," I said.

"I think you need to sit him down and talk to him," Marie said.

I knew Marie was right, but I really didn't want to. I didn't want to fight with Maddox. And, if I was being really honest, I didn't want to hear about how he'd never really loved me. Anger was an easier emotion to deal with. I'd already had my heart broken by him. If he said anything to me about not caring about me when he'd left, I didn't think my heart could handle it. Even after all these years.

"Well, I think you need to just keep screwing each other's brains out," Darcy said.

I felt like I was a cartoon who had the devil on one shoulder and an angel on the other. Except mine were two friends, and one was telling me to talk while the other was telling me to have sex. The image of my two friends sitting on my shoulders, whispering, *Talk*, and, *Have sex*, in my ears made me laugh.

That was a hell of a lot better than feeling sorry for myself.

We finished lunch and spent the rest of the afternoon shopping. I had dinner at Marie's house, and she offered to let me stay the night, but I had an eight a.m. appointment, so I opted to drive home.

When I got back to Brook Creek, I parked Pete's car

behind his building and dropped off the keys. I walked down to my place, so lost in thought that I almost didn't see Maddox step out of the shadows and approach me.

I knew Marie was right on some level, but Maddox and I weren't a couple. We weren't falling in love again, and we weren't going to. I had a feeling there was just too much standing in our way even if we wanted to.

I held out my hand. He slipped his in mine, and I led him up the stairs.

For now, our bodies could do the talking. It was good enough for me.

16

MADDOX

I brushed Addison's brown hair off her neck as she lay, sleeping on my arm.

"Oh, Addy, what am I going to do with you?"

She smiled in her sleep, as if she'd heard me.

After my brother had gotten over his embarrassment last evening, he'd lectured me about messing with Addison Graham. He'd reminded me that nothing good could come from it.

I'd just ignored him and gone back to what I'd been working on before Addison interrupted me. But, inside, I was worried that part of him was right.

That was why I could never fall for her again.

I remembered giving myself the same speech about never having sex with her again the night I had come to town. But sex and love were two different things.

And she was the best goddamn fuck I'd ever had.

I didn't understand it. Out of all the women I'd been with over the years—and I'd been with a lot—she was still at the top of the list.

Addison snuggled closer to me, and I closed my eyes for a minute and let myself enjoy being next to her.

But, when I felt sleep tugging me down, I quickly opened my eyes. If I were here in the morning, it would give her the wrong idea.

I gently rolled Addison off my arm, careful not to wake her, and pulled myself from her body. My wet dick protested leaving the warmth of her heat and smacked me on the stomach in retaliation.

Fucking prick. Pun intended.

I slowly got out of bed, and as I got dressed, I watched the first and only girl I'd ever loved sleep.

If things had gone the way we'd planned, I wouldn't have to be sneaking out of her room. We'd be lying in the bed we shared together. Maybe a kid or two would be sleeping down the hall from us.

Fucking life was a bitch.

I really shouldn't be thinking about that now.

It made me want to wake Addison and shake her for leaving me hanging when I had gone down for the robbery and murder. And, at the same time, I wanted to fall to my knees and beg for an answer as to why she hadn't been there for me. I had needed her.

Idiot.

I needed to get out of there ASAP. I'd worked hard on not being bitter, and I wasn't going to start now.

As I left Addison's and went next door to my own place, I focused on how lucky I was. Sure, I'd lost Addison, but I'd gained a lot. I'd worked at a job I loved for years. I might have gotten a scholarship for football to go to college, but I had known I was never good enough to go pro. I would have ended up working in some office job that I would have hated.

Instead, I had gotten paid to work out, spend time with friends, and blow shit up. My life could have turned out a lot worse.

I grabbed a beer from the fridge. Then, I pulled my phone from my pocket and dialed Flash.

"Miss me already?" he answered.

Of course I did, but I couldn't say that out loud. "Fuck no."

Flash laughed. "Same here, buddy."

"I didn't wake you, did I?"

Flash was an hour later than me, and he had to work tomorrow.

"No. I was just watching TV. How's it going there?"

"Okay."

"Have you seen her yet?"

"Addison?" I swiped my hand down my face. "Yeah."

"Did you ask the bitch why she'd left you hanging all those years ago?"

I winced at his term for Addison. "Dude, don't call her that, okay? And, no, the topic hasn't come up."

The other end of the line was silent.

I pulled my phone away and looked at it to make sure my call hadn't dropped. I put it back to my ear. "Flash?"

"*Fuck me.*"

"What?"

"You fucked her, didn't you?"

I sighed.

"Goddamn it. I'm right." I heard movement on the other side of the call. "What are you thinking? She doesn't care about anyone but herself."

"I didn't propose to the woman. I just had sex with her. I have had sex before and not professed my love."

"Yeah, to girls who just wanted to screw you for your uniform. This Addison…she's trouble."

I had to laugh at the *trouble* term. He sounded like a parent who didn't want their child hanging out with the kid with the bad reputation. "Okay, Mom."

"Fuck you, dude."

"Anything exciting happen since I left?" I asked, changing the subject.

"There's talk that we might be heading out soon."

I closed my eyes and imagined that I would be going with. When we were on a mission, there was no time to think about anything but the objective. I wouldn't have time to think about Addison, this stupid town, or all the looks I had gotten on Saturday night for coming back when no one wanted me here but my family.

"Do you know where yet?"

"Nah, nobody's said, so it's probably just a training exercise."

"I wish I were going with."

"Regretting retirement? You've been there only a couple of days."

"Don't remind me."

"You're going to go help your brother at his garage tomorrow, right?"

"Yeah. I was over there today for a few hours already."

"That should help."

"I hope so. This town sucks."

Flash laughed. "You need to let them know that they have one of the best petty officers the Navy has ever spit out there. You're better than they give you credit for." Flash cleared his throat. We never got too emotional with each other, so it was always uncomfortable. "Your mom was glad to see you though, right?"

I smiled. "Yes, she was."

"That's good. Say, when I get some leave, I was thinking I should come visit."

"Wouldn't you rather go and visit your family?"

"Nah. My parents are coming next month."

I wanted Flash to come here more than anything. "Well, if you're bored, you're always welcome to come visit."

Flash laughed. "I'll keep you posted."

"Sounds good."

"Until then, stay away from the magic pussy."

"Magic pussy?"

"That Addison chick must have a magic pussy for you to hop into bed with her after everything."

"Her pussy is just a regular pussy."

"Whatever you say. Talk to you later."

"Later."

I hung up the phone, feeling a little better.

I wondered what Addison would think if I told her she had a magic pussy.

17

ADDISON

Tuesday morning, I woke up, alone, and although I was surprised, I found myself disappointed. It was stupid to feel that way.

After a quick breakfast, I went and dropped off my car at the garage. I was relieved to see that Foster wasn't in yet, and I quickly handed my keys to the receptionist, an elderly lady by the name of Sally, at the counter before heading to my office, catching a ride from Serena.

Once there, I turned on the lights, changed the sign to Open, and pulled out the files I needed for the day.

Serena walked in the door right a minute behind me as my phone rang, so I answered it myself.

"Addison Graham's office. Addison speaking," I said as I sat down behind my desk.

"Addison, I don't know what you said to your father, but he finally said yes!"

I frowned. "Brandon?"

"Yes, it's me."

"My father said yes to what?"

"The golf course."

I jumped up from my seat, knocking over my chair. "Shut the front door! You're joking, right?"

Serena came to my doorway with a questioning look on her face, and I smiled to let her know everything was good.

"So, you didn't say anything to your dad?"

"No. I figured it was hopeless after our last conversation."

I'd been working on trying to get a golf course built in our town for about two years now. I had met Brandon almost five years ago, and we dated for a year and a half. Over time, it got hard to have a long-distance relationship, especially after the newness wore off. But we remained friends, and when he went to work for a new employer that was into the development of golf courses, Brandon suggested our little town as a place to build one.

We might be a small town, but we had a lot of other small towns around us. I had no doubt a golf course would bring in revenue to Brook Creek and offer jobs.

Years ago, people had liked living in small towns, but they'd lost their novelty with the last few generations, and sometimes, our economy struggled. I thought it would be a great way to help the people here.

The bad part was that my father owned the land, and he flat-out said no. He barely listened to Brandon's presentation. I didn't know if it was because my father had never been a huge fan of Brandon's—although he'd take Brandon over Maddox any day—or if it was because I'd brought the idea to him. Either way, my father had said no.

I'd tried to bring it up every few months, but the last time I had asked about it, my father had been so mad, I thought he was going to have another stroke. I'd let it go after that.

My father's one-eighty surprised me just as much as it had Brandon.

"We're doing a phone conference later this afternoon to work out the details, but it sounds like it's a go."

"This is amazing. You have to let me know what happens after this afternoon's phone call."

"You won't be there?"

"I'm thinking it's best that I stay away. Whatever has my father changing his mind, I don't want to reverse that decision by reminding him that he was against the project in the beginning."

Brandon laughed. "You and your father have an odd relationship."

"Tell me about it."

"I'll call you later."

"Thanks." I hung up the phone and pumped my fists in the air a few times. I was sure I looked like a dork, but I didn't care.

"What happened?" Serena asked.

I turned and grabbed my chair from the floor. "Remember the golf course project I told you about?"

"The one your dad keeps squashing?"

I sat down and pushed myself to my desk. "That one. My father apparently called up the developer and said he'd changed his mind."

"Wow. That's amazing."

"It is. It'll help out our little town so much. I know it'll take some time to complete the project, but once it's done, it'll offer so many jobs to everyone."

"I'm so happy for you."

"Happy for us. You're part of this town, too."

Serena grinned. "Happy for us then."

"I think, no matter what happens the rest of the day, it won't bring me down."

My phone rang again. Serena was still standing in my office, so I told her, "It's okay. I've got it."

"You're not going to need me anymore if you keep answering your own phone."

I laughed and picked up the receiver. "Addison Graham."

"Addison," Maddox's gravelly voice said. It didn't sound that different from last night when he'd said my name in my ear as he came inside me.

"Yes?" I said as tingles went down my spine. I tried to act casual in front of his niece. I didn't want her to see my reaction to any of her uncle's dirty talk.

Thankfully, Serena turned around and went into the main room.

"You need a new timing belt."

Well, that was a double disappointment. I hadn't known Maddox was working at his brother's place. He'd only called to deliver bad news.

"A timing belt? And here I thought you called me to whisper nasty things in my ear."

"You want me to talk filthy to you? How's this? It'll cost about eight hundred dollars."

I slumped back in my chair. "You need to work on your dirty talk."

Maddox laughed.

"So, this is something that needs to be done?" I sighed. I was going to have to really budget my money this month.

"Do you know anything about cars?"

"No. And I'm not ashamed to admit it."

"Your timing belt is not something to mess with. If it goes out while you're driving, it could ruin your engine. And it's also a safety thing. You don't want to be driving it if it breaks."

"Okay. Will it be done today?"

"You have somewhere you need to be?"

"No, but I hate being vehicle-less." I tilted my head. "I suppose I can always ask Pete if I can borrow his again if I need to."

Of course, then Pete would be without a car. It wasn't the best solution.

A deep groan sounded from the other side of the phone. "I'll take you wherever you need to go," Maddox said with a little bit of a bite.

This was interesting.

"Even if I have to go to the OB/GYN?"

"I've seen guys get blown up and body parts scattered in pieces. You're not going to gross me out by talking about going to the lady doctor."

"Okay, but I don't even know your phone number."

"I live next door."

"What if you're not home?"

He rattled off some numbers. Thankfully, I was in my office with plenty of paper and pens.

"Got it. Do you want mine?"

"I already have it."

I frowned.

"It's in the computer."

"Oh. Right. Okay then. Someone will call me when it's done?"

"Yes."

"Thank you."

"Welcome. And, Addison?"

"Yeah?"

"Tonight, I'm going to bend you over your bed and fuck you from behind. Then, I'm going to put you on your knees and come in your mouth. Be prepared."

My mouth dropped open as I heard a click on the other side of the line.

Maybe Maddox didn't need to work on his dirty talk after all.

The shiver was back.

I couldn't wait.

18

MADDOX

Wednesday morning, a phone call woke me from my sleep. I blindly reached my hand to my nightstand and hit the volume button to quiet the noise.

I was just falling back asleep when there was pounding at my door.

"What the fuck?" I flipped the covers back and stomped to the door. I whipped it open as I said, "What the hell do you want?"

Addison screeched and covered her eyes. "Maddox, you're naked."

I laughed as I grabbed the arm she wasn't using to hide her face and pulled her inside. "Stop acting like you haven't seen everything already. I still smell like you, for Christ's sake." I shut the door behind her.

She peeked at me through her fingers. "Can you get dressed? I need a ride."

I crossed my arms over my chest and studied her. She was wearing some sort of gray suit. She had on a blouse, a jacket, and a knee-length skirt. She looked professional. And hot. It brought to mind all my naughty schoolteacher fantasies.

"Maddox, you need to put on some clothes."

"Why?"

"You can't drive naked, and"—she pointed to my crotch with her free hand—"you're getting hard."

"I'll give you a ride, but it's going to cost you."

She dropped the hand over her face and frowned. "You never said anything about a fee."

"That was before you woke me up at"—I looked at my wrist where my diving watch sat—"six seventeen in the morning." I put my arm down and caught her staring at my dick.

She quickly looked up to my face, her cheeks turning red. She lifted her chin. "What do you want?"

"You know what I want, baby."

"I'm not sucking your dick again."

That made me laugh.

"What's so funny about that?"

I took a step closer to Addison and twirled her around. I got behind her and put my hands on her shoulders. I slid my hands down her arms until I got to her hands, which I picked up and placed on the wall.

"I laughed because, last night, you acted like my cock was the best goddamn lollipop you'd ever tasted in your life," I said next to her ear as I rubbed my dick on her ass. Her hair was up on the top of her head, giving me easy access to her neck.

I gently bit down, and she moaned.

I dropped down to my haunches, reached underneath her skirt, and pulled her panties down. "Step out," I told her. "Keep your hands on the wall."

She lifted each high heel, and I slipped her underwear off and threw them across the room.

She gasped.

"You don't need those." I skimmed my hand up the inside of her leg. "Are you wet?"

She looked down at me from over her shoulder. She bit her lip and nodded.

"You like sucking me off, don't you?"

"Maybe."

I lightly brushed my fingers over her cleft and stood. "Fucking liar. There's no maybe about it," I said, and I thrust into her. "Wet. Just the way I like you."

I pulled out until just the tip of me was still inside her, and then I grabbed her hips and pulled her back to me. I directed her body away and back to me a few more times.

"Fuck me. Just like that."

Addison shifted in her seat for the twentieth time. "I don't think it's fair that I couldn't put my underwear back on."

I draped my hand over the steering wheel. "I never said you couldn't. I said you could put them on if you found them."

She narrowed her eyes at me. "After you hid them from me."

I shrugged. "You shouldn't be covering up that pretty pussy with panties." I squinted my eyes at the road coming up. "Where do we turn again?"

"Hundred and Sixty-Seventh Street. Make a right."

We were on the highway, going at full speed, so I slowed

when we came to the next street. It said 167th, and I turned right.

"It'll be the first house on the right. It's about half a mile down."

House was a modest word for the dilapidated structure that sat on the overgrown lawn full of weeds. It stood on at least a couple of acres, but it looked like the land wasn't used for anything, going by the lack of care. I parked next to a beat-up car, and the two of us exited my SUV.

The front door opened to the house before we even reached the steps.

"Addison," a little boy around four or five yelled. He ran down the stairs and into her arms.

She picked him up. "Where's your mommy, Ben?"

"She's in the bathroom, crying." He put a finger to his lips. "Don't tell. She thinks I don't know."

Addison looked over the boy's head with worry in her eyes. "That's why I'm here, buddy." She set him on the ground.

"Who's that?" Ben asked.

"That's my friend."

I snorted.

"His name is Maddox."

I lifted my sunglasses off my face and set them on the top of my head. "How's it going, Ben?"

"You're huge," he said with amazement in his eyes.

"That's what she said."

Addison's arm whipped out and smacked me in the stomach. She shook her hand and rubbed her knuckles.

I grinned.

"You two are funny," Ben said.

"You think so?" I asked.

Ben laughed. "Yeah." He grabbed both our hands and led us inside. "Mommy, Addison's here. And she brought a friend for me to play with."

I raised an eyebrow, and Addison snickered.

A door opened, and a very young woman came out of what I assumed to be the bathroom. She looked way too young to have a kid as old as Ben.

When she saw me, she paused in her tracks. Her eyes were filled with fear.

"Claire, this is Maddox. I know he looks scary."

Scary?

I didn't look scary.

"But he's a nice guy." She looked at me and whispered, "When he wants to be."

I smiled at this, and Claire looked a little more at ease.

I held up my hands. "I mean you no harm, miss. I just came along to give Addison a ride."

"And to play with me," Ben said.

I grinned. "And to play with Ben." I looked at Addison. "Take your time. I'll call Foster and tell him I'll be in late."

"Thank you," she said with genuine sincerity in her eyes. "Should we go in the kitchen?" she asked Claire.

Ben pulled on my arm. "Come on, we can go to my room. We can play soldier." He took off to the end of a short hallway.

"Do you have any Navy SEALs?" I called after him as I followed him down the hall.

19

ADDISON

I stared out the window of Maddox's SUV, wishing there were something more I could do for Claire. I was kind of a jack-of-all-trades lawyer, and she needed someone in family law. Someone who was ruthless and good.

I reached into my purse and pulled out the small notebook I kept on hand. I doubted I would forget about Claire, but I added, *Call family lawyers about pro bono,* to the list anyway.

"Are you okay?" Maddox asked.

I turned my head to look at him. "No."

"You want to talk about it?"

"Do you remember Mickey Williams at all? He was from Elkton and a couple of years younger than us."

Elkton was one of Brook Creek's neighboring towns.

"I think I remember him. Cocky little shit?"

"Yeah. And he turned into an asshole adult." I proceeded to tell Maddox common knowledge or things he would be able to look up at the local courthouse. I wasn't going to break attorney-client privilege. "He met Claire while she was a freshman at Iowa State. Knocked her up, convinced her to drop out of college and move here, so they could get married."

"That explains why she looks so young."

"Yeah, she was eighteen when Mickey married her and brought her here. Once the baby was born, he ditched Claire and Ben and filed for divorce. She's been struggling to make ends meet for almost five years. Meanwhile, Mickey's been living who knows where and getting paid under the table."

"What a dick."

"Just wait. He finally turned up a few months ago with a legit job, and now, he owes Claire a buttload of back child support. I've been helping her for free, giving her legal advice, just being an ear for her when she needs it. This morning, she called me in a panic. She's young, and she can sometimes overreact, so I wasn't too worried when I came to get you this morning."

"But?"

"But, apparently, Mickey doesn't want to pay child support, and he's going to sue her for sole custody."

Maddox swore. "Can he do that?"

"There's nothing stopping him."

"I mean, can he win? Can he get sole custody?"

"Iowa tends to favor the mother, but I'm scared for her. She's a waitress with weird hours, and it looks like Mickey has a really good job. It also looks like he remarried recently, which would give Ben a two-parent home."

"So, this prick hasn't seen his kid for over four years. He essentially doesn't want to take care of his kid by paying child support, and now, he's going to sue her for sole custody —in which case, he'd have to take care of his kid."

I laughed. "Yeah, ironic. Except he doesn't really want

custody. He wants Claire to not go after him for child support."

"He hit her, too, didn't he?"

I was sure my face was full of surprise. "How did you know?"

His hand tightened on the steering wheel for a second. "She seemed scared of me."

I looked Maddox over. It wasn't like I didn't notice his height, broad shoulders, thick biceps, and big hands, but a part of him was still the boy I'd known in high school. I could see how his imposing figure would scare someone like Claire.

"Yeah, he was a real piece of work. Him leaving was the best and worst thing to happen to Claire."

"What happened to her family?"

"They disowned her when she got pregnant and dropped out of college. She's basically stuck with living here, too. She can't sell the house or land because Mickey's name is still on the deed. She gets to live rent-free, but she's trapped in this small town." She was one of the reasons I wanted the golf course to be built. It would give Claire and others like her better job opportunities. I rubbed my forehead. I could feel the mother of all headaches coming on. "I just hope I can find some way to help her."

"You really care about her, don't you?"

I dropped my hand. "Of course. I care about all my clients." I didn't understand where this revelation of his was coming from.

A look of sadness crossed Maddox's face.

"You okay?"

He took a deep breath and nodded. "Yeah."

I put my hand on his arm. "You sure?"

"Yeah."

His bicep flexed under my fingers, and he flinched like he didn't want my hand there, so I removed it.

I reclined my seat, suddenly tired. We had about five to ten minutes before we got back to my office since Claire lived right outside of town. I watched Maddox through my half-closed lids as I lay back and relaxed.

Back in high school, when we drove around and I got tired, I would lie down with my head in his lap. His old pickup had had a bench seat perfect for sleeping—among other things.

I let my eyes drift shut and tried not to think of days gone by. I didn't know if it was harder to cope when Maddox wasn't around or when he was sitting right next to me.

I dozed a bit and woke when I felt the SUV stop and the engine turn off. I pulled the lever to move my seat back up but sat there for a minute. I was going to have to make a lot of phone calls once I walked into my building.

My door opened, and Maddox squatted next to the vehicle. I hadn't even noticed he'd already gotten out of the car.

"Hey," he said.

"Hey."

God, he is so handsome.

He gently took my legs and swung me, so I was facing him. He lifted each of my ankles, one at a time, and then I felt the fabric of my underwear touch my calves and shins.

Maddox slowly slid them up my lower limbs. "Lift."

I arched my back so that he could push my panties up and over my butt.

"Where were they?" I asked.

He smirked. "In my pocket."

"You are such an ass."

He smiled and pulled me forward. I was still on the seat, so I had to look down on him. I pushed a lock of dark blond hair from his forehead. I remembered when I used to run my fingers through it. It was so short now.

"What are you thinking about?" he whispered.

I quickly pulled my hand away. I didn't want him to know how much I'd missed him, even when he was right in front of me.

"Nothing," I said and tried to smile.

Maddox's eyes turned hard, and he straightened. He offered his hand, and I used it to get out of the car.

"Have a good day, Addison," he said as he quickly walked to his side of the vehicle.

I closed my door. "Okay." I didn't understand the change in behavior. "You, too."

He waved a hand in a sort of half-salute but didn't look at me. And, when he got in his SUV, he took off like the hounds of hell were coming for him.

20

MADDOX

Later that night, I knocked on my sister's front door.

"Come in," Kelly called from the other side.

I entered the modest ranch house and looked around. My sister had done okay for herself since I was gone. Her home was small and the furniture older, but it was clean, and whatever she was cooking in the kitchen smelled delicious.

"Hey," she said, peeking her head around the corner. "I'm just finishing up. Come help me."

"What do you need help with?" I asked when I walked into the room.

She handed me a bowl of mashed potatoes. "Put this on the table, will ya?"

"No problem."

"Serena, come and set the table," she yelled too close to my ear.

I rubbed my offended drum. "Damn, that was loud."

She laughed. "Sorry."

"No, you're not."

She smiled over her shoulder.

Serena walked into the kitchen. "Uncle Maddox, you made it."

I loved how this kid's face lit up when she saw me. "Sure did. Why would I want to miss this?"

She beamed. "You wouldn't. Mom makes the best pot roast in town."

"So, that's what smells so good."

"Serena, table," Kelly reminded her daughter. "You can put the beans on the table, Maddox."

"What do you want to drink, Uncle Maddox?"

"I'll take a beer if you have one."

Kelly shook her head. "We don't have any alcohol in this house."

"Because of when Mom visits?" I asked.

"Because I don't want to be like her," Kelly said.

I wanted to tell my sister I was proud of her, but her shoulders were squared, and I could tell she didn't want me commenting.

"I'll just take a water, please," I told Serena.

A few minutes later, we sat down to eat.

"Thanks for having me over."

"Yeah, well, you're my little brother. I can't be mad at you forever."

"Love you, too, sis." I looked at Serena. "So, what have you been up to this week? Having fun on your summer vacation?"

Her eyes rounded with excitement. "Well, since Addison took the day off on Monday, I went to the beach with my friends. And then yesterday—"

"Hold up. What does Addison have to do with anything?"

My sister looked guilty, but Serena didn't seem to notice.

"I work for her," my niece said.

I swung my head toward Kelly.

She shrugged. "It's a good gig. She pays Serena well and is flexible. She's going to let Serena stay on when she goes to class this fall."

Serena's face grew grim. "What's wrong with me working for Addison?" she asked, confused.

I narrowed my eyes at my sister. She knew Addison had ditched me all those years ago, and she'd let her daughter go and work for the woman.

"What the fuck?"

Kelly narrowed her eyes. "Language. And stop looking at me like that. I know you gave Addison a ride today. I know your car isn't the only thing she's riding."

I sat back in my chair.

"Don't look surprised. This is Brook Creek, remember? Everyone knows what everyone else is doing."

I scowled back. "I know I gave her a ride. It's just..." I still felt betrayed. It was one thing for me to involve myself with my ex-girlfriend, but I was hurt that Kelly had let Serena go work for Addison without any regard as to how I'd feel.

It especially stung after what had happened when I brought Addison home this morning. There was a moment when she was playing with my hair that I thought she was remembering us together. I almost kissed her. Something I'd been avoiding doing since I came back in town, even when we had sex. Kissing involved something more than just sex did.

But, when I asked Addison what she was thinking about, she responded with nothing. I'd thought she'd wrung all the pain she could from me, but there I'd been, with a fresh wound.

Serena's revelation was like pouring salt into it.

My sister sighed and looked apologetic. She set her fork, tongs down, on her plate. "Look, I'm sorry. I know she wasn't there for you when you needed her. But I had to think about Serena first. And it's not like you were around to ask. Please try to understand."

I took a deep breath. I couldn't stay mad. "I understand. Please, next time, tell me, so I'm not blindsided like that."

Kelly nodded at the same time Serena said, "What are you two talking about?" She was eyeing the two of us like we were going to tell her something bad.

I smiled at my niece. "Nothing. It was a long time ago." I took another bite of food and swallowed. "Continue with your story. What else were you going to say?"

Serena's grin returned. "Well, Tuesday, Addison got a phone call that a project she'd been working on was going to happen."

"Oh, yeah? What's that?"

"Some big company is going to build a golf course here. It'll open up jobs for the community and bring in revenue to our town."

"You sound like a brochure," Kelly said.

Serena shrugged. "I'm just repeating what Addison said."

"A golf course, huh? That should be fun."

My sister's jaw dropped. "You play golf now?"

"Fu—" I looked at my niece. "Hell no. But it might be fun for others."

Serena laughed. "You're funny, Uncle Maddox."

"Thanks. I think."

"So, Addison didn't tell you any of this?" Serena asked.

"I think they're too busy for work talk," Kelly said.

I shot her a look. I knew Serena was eighteen, but still, she didn't need to hear about her uncle's sex life. Or her boss's.

"Um, no. Addison was preoccupied with one of her clients I took her to see this morning. We didn't really discuss anything else. Then, she went to work, and so did I. I didn't see her the rest of the day."

Serena shrugged. "Oh, well, you'll have to ask her about it sometime."

"I might do that. But I don't think it'll be anytime soon. Her car is going to be ready tomorrow." I looked at Kelly. "I won't be giving her any more *rides*."

That night, after I returned home from dinner, I stayed strong. I didn't give Addison's place a second look as I went upstairs to my own.

21

ADDISON

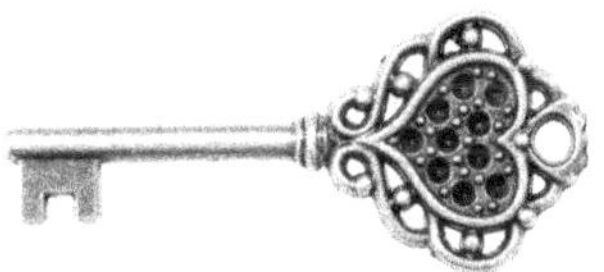

Thursday started out like all my mornings the last few years had. Alone.

I'd heard Maddox come home last night, and I had lain in bed for what felt like hours, but he never came to visit me. I'd even gone to bed early in preparation for some hot sex.

When he hadn't shown, I'd been upset, and then I was freaked out that I was upset. The man hadn't even been back in town for a week, and I was already planning things in my life around him. Hadn't I already learned that he couldn't be counted on?

Thank God I didn't have any panicked phone calls this morning, and I didn't need to go anywhere that I couldn't walk to. Although, at this point, I would ask someone else if I could borrow their car before I asked Maddox to take me anywhere.

I went downstairs to work and tried to put all men out of my mind. I made a few more phone calls for Claire, and by the time I was done, I'd found three firms who were willing to take her on as a pro bono case. I lined up meetings for the following week for each of them to meet Claire with me present, and I prayed that one of them would be the perfect fit.

For lunch, Serena brought both of us roast beef sandwiches. I loved it when Kelly made roast beef because Serena would bring leftovers the next day. They were always so delicious.

And, even though it was just some phone calls and good food, I was starting to feel better about the day. It reminded me that I'd lived without Maddox Wolfe in my life for twelve years, and a few nights of hot sex didn't change that.

But then five thirty rolled around, and as I was just finishing up work, the phone rang.

"Addison Graham's office. How may I help you?" Serena said from the front room. She paused and then said, "Okay, I will let her know," in a professional voice, and I had to smile. Serena sighed, and now, her voice was a little less professional as she said, "Yes, I'll tell her." She said, "Bye," and hung up the phone.

A few seconds later, Serena got up and came to my office. "I'm supposed to tell you, your car's finished."

I smiled. She must have been talking to one of her uncles. That would explain the unprofessional voice.

"Great."

The day was turning out even better. It would feel so freeing to be able to drive myself again. I laughed at myself. I hadn't gone that long without a set of wheels.

I noticed that Serena was still standing in front of my desk.

"Sorry, did you say anything else? I was lost in thought."

"No."

But she didn't leave.

"Is there something else you wanted to say?"

Serena looked down at her nails. "I was just wondering. Why was Uncle Maddox so mad when he found out I worked for you?"

I could feel my good mood slowly slipping away. I sat back in my chair to get a better look at my assistant. "What do you mean, he was mad?"

"He said, 'What the fuck?' when he found out. Then, he and my mom got into an argument. But, when I asked them why, he said, 'It was a long time ago.'"

"Oh, he did, did he?"

"Yeah, I don't get it. Because my mom and him also made references to you two doing it, like I'm some kid who doesn't know what sex is. But I don't understand why my uncle would be having sex with you when he's obviously mad at you. Although he made it clear that it wasn't going to happen again."

Serena was kind of confusing me.

"So, let me get this clear. Maddox found out that you worked for me and he got mad?"

"Pissed." She nodded. "*Pissed* would be a better word."

"Okay, so he got pissed. And then he said the reason was because of something that happened a long time ago?"

"Yep."

"And, to finish it off, he said he wasn't...going to sleep with me again."

"Yes. Although he actually said he wasn't going to give you any more rides. He said your car would be fixed today, but I know he meant other rides."

That son of a bitch. He was making me out to be the bad guy.

The phone rang again, and Serena ran to answer it. "Hello?" Sigh. "Okay, I'll tell her." Sigh. "I said I would. Goodbye."

She came back in. "Uh…that was Maddox, and he said that the shop closes at six and won't be open again until Monday, so if you want your car, you'd better go and get it."

"Since when are they closed on Friday and Saturday?"

She shrugged. "He must really be mad at you."

What an asshole.

"Uh, Addison?"

"Yeah."

"It's already after five forty. You might want to go."

"Fucker," I said under my breath as I grabbed my purse and ran out the door.

The garage wasn't that far away, minutes in the car, but running in high heels gave me only seconds to spare by the time I got to the door.

"Oh, good," Sally said. "I was told you'd be coming, but I didn't know if you'd make it on time, and I need to go and pick up my husband."

I didn't say anything because I was too busy catching my breath, but I pulled out my card and handed it over for her to run.

I signed the receipt, and Sally handed me the keys and my card. I shoved both in my purse.

"Thanks, dear," she said as she grabbed her own handbag.

"Hey, are you really closed tomorrow and Saturday?"

Sally frowned. "No. Why would we be closed?"

Inside, I was seething. It took every bit of control I had to ask, "Is Maddox still here?" as calmly as possible.

"Oh, yeah. He's in the back."

"Do you mind…" I pointed to the back.

"Go ahead. I'll see you later, Addison."

"Later."

I waited until Sally was at her car before I stomped to the back of the garage.

"Maddox," I yelled, not seeing him anywhere.

He came out of the back office, wearing cargo pants and a T-shirt. "What?" he said with a look of scorn when he saw me, as if he were the one who had a right to be mad at me.

I was so furious; I didn't know what else to do with my anger. I dropped my purse on the floor, walked over, and slapped him.

Maddox slowly turned his head back to face me. The fire in his eyes should have had me running for the door, but there was a part of me that knew, no matter what had happened between us, he'd never hurt me.

He grabbed me around the waist and threw me over his shoulder. I kicked and hit him the best I could, but he held my legs, and my hands probably felt like pebbles as they hit his big muscles.

He dropped me down on my ass onto the open bed of a truck and stuck a finger in my face. "You get to do that once. Don't ever hit me again unless you're willing to suffer the consequences."

That was exactly the wrong thing to say to me, and reacting on pure instinct, I raised my other hand and slapped him again.

"You're going to fucking get it."

"I dare you."

Maddox pulled my legs toward him, and my upper body fell backward. I caught my head before it hit the truck bed, but my back took the brunt of the fall.

"Ooph."

Maddox took off one of my heels, and it went flying. Then, he did the same with its partner. I tried to kick him.

"What the hell are you doing?"

"Teaching you a lesson."

Maddox trapped my leg between his and the truck.

"What are you going to do? Spank me?"

He stopped what he was doing and tilted his head. "I was just going to fuck you, but now that you say that, a spanking might serve your spoiled ass right."

I sat up and beat on his chest a couple of times. "You asshole. I'm not a spoiled brat."

Maddox practically ignored me and flipped me over. He pulled down my pants and underwear to my knees and swatted my ass.

"*Motherfucker,*" I yelled. I scowled at him over my shoulder. "That hurt."

"Good."

Smack.

"*Ouch.*"

Despite the pain, I could feel myself getting wet, and I wanted him to do it again.

He rolled me back over and removed my pants and underwear in one quick swoop.

"What are you doing?"

"I changed my mind. Spankings are for good girls. You were starting to like that too much."

He ripped open his pants and pulled me off the edge of the truck bed and straight onto his hard cock.

22

MADDOX

I loved watching a woman's back arch as she adjusted to my size. But not as much as I loved watching Addison's pussy swallow my cock whole.

Back when I'd taken her virginity, it'd taken her over a month before she could take all of me inside her. Pushing inside her now reminded me of that. Except, while she was still tight, I could slide all the way home into her sweet heat.

"Oh God, Maddox."

"Yeah? You like that?"

I watched where our bodies met each time I pulled out of her pussy lips, which hugged the sides of my dick. God, I fucking loved that.

"Do you like me being inside you, Addison?"

"Yes."

"Why'd you slap me?"

"Because you're an asshole."

I laughed. She wasn't wrong.

I grabbed her hand and pulled her up into my arms. I picked her up, keeping our bodies connected.

Addison wrapped her arms around my neck. "What are you doing?"

"Moving you somewhere I can fuck you properly." I laid her down on the hood of the car next to us. I brushed her hair from her face. "What is it about you that makes me so crazy?"

Her pussy squeezed around my dick.

"I don't know, but it's the same for me."

I growled at her admission and slipped an arm under her knee to spread her wider. I wanted to be inside her as far as possible. I wanted to leave my mark on her. When I was with her, I wanted things I couldn't even explain.

I thrust inside her like a man gone wild, watching her writhe on my dick and moan as she got closer to coming.

I dropped down, so our chests were touching, taking her leg with me, opening her up even further.

She panted in my ear as I sucked on her neck. My thrusts picked up speed and intensity. The only sounds in the garage were the echo of our bodies smacking each other.

Addison turned her mouth toward me and moaned loudly. Then, she sucked my earlobe into her mouth and scraped her teeth against it. She let go. "Right there. Please, Maddox." She was clawing at my back, her hands under my tee. "Please. Right there. I'm going to come. I'm going to come."

She didn't need to tell me with words. I knew she was about to blow. Her pussy was dripping and gripping me so tight. But her dirty talk was a fucking turn-on for me. And hearing her say my name made me want to make her mine.

I moved my mouth down her neck and shoved the open collar of her shirt aside. I sucked on the hot skin there.

"Oh-oh-oh, fuck," Addison screamed as she came.

I bit down on her shoulder as I shoved my cock inside her one last time and let all my frustrations go.

The orgasm was intense, and I felt as if I'd left my body. When I came back to myself, Addison's hand was in my hair, and her one leg was wrapped around me.

I felt her pussy pulse every few seconds around me, and I tasted blood in my mouth. My back hurt, and it felt sticky.

I felt like I didn't know what day of the week it was.

I pushed myself up onto my hands and looked down at Addison. Her leg that I'd been holding between us slipped down to my side.

"Are you okay?" I asked as I stared at the red and bleeding bite mark. It was just a trickle of blood, but I couldn't believe I'd bitten her so hard.

"Um…yeah." She shifted around a bit. "My back is a little sore."

I stood and pulled out of her. I watched the whiteness of my seed slide out of her, and it made me hard again. I wanted all of it inside her.

I used my finger to gather up the little that had escaped. "Open," I said.

She parted her lips, and I placed my digit at her mouth.

"Suck."

She stared into my eyes as she grabbed my hand with both of hers and sucked me clean.

I ripped my hand away and kissed her. I pushed my tongue into her mouth. I wanted to know what the two of us tasted like together, too.

This was the first time I'd kissed her in twelve years, and I felt like I was falling. Falling to I didn't know where, but I knew I wasn't going to be the same.

I wanted to make love to her again, but I heard the sound of a car outside, so I reluctantly let her go.

I buttoned and zipped up my fatigues as I went to grab her clothes. I found her pants, panties, and shoes not far and brought them back to her. As I helped her put them on, I said, "I'm sorry for biting you. You can send me the dry-cleaning bill."

She put her hand on her neck. "Oh. Okay."

I helped her stand now that she was completely dressed. "Why did you really slap me?" I asked. My voice was surprisingly calm. I realized I wasn't mad anymore.

She winced. "I'm sorry. I shouldn't have done that."

"You didn't answer why."

She looked down at her hands and sighed. "Serena told me what you'd said last night." She looked up at me and smiled. "By the way, you do realize your niece is eighteen, right? She knew you and your sister were talking about sex."

I smiled, too. "I sometimes forget." I took Addison's hand in mine and pulled her close. "Forget what I said last night. I've decided I can't stay away from you. And I don't want to. We're never going to be what we once were, but that doesn't mean we can't enjoy each other."

I had no idea what she was thinking. A whole range of emotions crossed her face—from confusion to hurt to anger again and back to confusion. "I think I'm—"

"Maddox, where are you?" Foster called from the doorway that separated the waiting room and receptionist desk from the back.

"I'm in here. Talking to Addison."

Foster walked into the work area. "I'm not interrupting anything, am I?"

I looked at Addison.

"No, I was just going."

I leaned down and kissed her cheek. "I'll see you tonight," I said in her ear.

She nodded once and then took off, swiping her purse off the floor before she went out the door.

"You okay, man?" Foster asked.

I felt like I'd been run over by a steamroller. "Yeah, why?"

"Because your back is bleeding."

I went to our tiny restroom and pulled off my shirt to look in the mirror. I had deep scratch marks down my back.

No wonder I felt the way I did.

Addison had marked me also. But I felt like hers was too close to my heart.

23

ADDISON

Sunday evening, it was dinner with my father again. Usually, we ate right away, but tonight, I was asked to come to my father's study. I figured he had some questions about the golf course project.

"Hey, Dad. Did you want to talk to me about something?"

My father looked up from behind his desk. "No, we're just waiting for someone else to join us. You know it's rude to sit down before all the guests have arrived."

I gritted my teeth. Of course I knew it was rude. But I hadn't known anyone else was coming. Sometimes, my father was a jerk.

The doorbell rang, and my father smiled.

He stood up and buttoned his suit jacket. "Let's go, shall we?"

Henry was just opening the door as Simon came into the foyer. Curious as to whom the mystery guest was, I stepped forward to greet them. It was usually only my father, Simon, and me for Sunday dinner.

"Brandon?"

My ex-boyfriend stood on the other side of the door, clearly feeling uncomfortable.

"Come in," my father said with sincerity.

I looked at him, wondering if he'd become ill. He didn't hate Brandon like he had Maddox, but he'd never been a big fan of his either.

Brandon walked into the room.

I stepped forward and kissed him on the cheek. "This is a surprise."

"For the both of us."

"What are you doing here?" I asked.

"I think your father will explain, but I do need to talk to you about something after dinner."

It sounded very ominous, but I could tell he didn't want to tell me in front of everyone. I nodded in understanding.

We took our seats at the dining room table with my father at the head, Simon on his right, me on his left, and Brandon next to me.

As the food was brought out to us, I watched Simon eye Brandon with disdain. I felt like I was in some sort of twilight zone. I didn't think Brandon and Simon had ever met.

I leaned closer to Brandon. "Do you and Simon know each other?"

He shook his head. "We just met earlier today."

"Why does he look like he hates you?"

"I have no idea."

It was strange, and I felt like I was missing something.

After our food was placed in front of us, my father spoke, "Addison, I have finally decided to move forward with the golf course development."

I mentally rolled my eyes. Naturally, my father thought I didn't know anything. It had been my idea in the first place, but he didn't think to include me or that anyone else would either. He was incredibly sexist, but I'd learned that it wasn't worth arguing about.

"That's magnificent." Feeding his ego got me a lot further in life.

"I've also decided that Brandon will be the head of the project."

"You decided?" I couldn't help but ask. Wouldn't it be his company's decision on whom they had direct the project? Did my father really think he had that much power?

"It was all part of our negotiation," my father explained. "I would only say yes if Brandon agreed to take control."

I looked at Brandon, and he shrugged. Last I'd heard, he was working on something else.

"And you agreed?"

"It felt like a stupid thing to say no to."

"Of course it would have been stupid," my father said.

But why?

I wanted to know. It was very weird that my father had requested Brandon for this. He had to be up to something.

We finished dinner with my father talking the whole time while Simon seethed from his seat, barely saying two words.

Toward the end, I could see my father was getting tired, although he'd never admit it. I wasn't his biggest admirer, but he was still my father, and I loved him.

"Dad, why don't you go finish up your work with Simon?" I offered. "I'll see Brandon out."

He tried to hide his relief, but I saw it all over his face.

Simon and my father left the dining room, and I took Brandon to the den.

"What's going on, Brandon?"

"I have no idea, Addison. All I know is that I got pulled off the project I had been working on, and I was told to come here."

"Isn't that weird?"

"A little. Sometimes, it happens when we're getting close to the end of one project and starting a new one, but I was in the middle of the last one."

"So, your boss didn't tell you why?"

"All he said was, your dad wanted me to head it up."

"Are you okay with it?" I asked.

"I'm fine. I think it's strange since your father never seemed to like me much."

"I thought the same thing."

"So, you admit your dad doesn't like me?"

I threw my hands up. "I honestly have no idea. He sure seemed happy to see you today. But don't feel bad. He's never liked anyone I've dated."

"I probably wouldn't either if I had a daughter."

"Yeah, except you wouldn't like it because no one would be good enough for her. My father doesn't like my boyfriends because no one is good enough for the Graham name." I waved my hand in front of me. "But we're getting off track. What did you want to talk to me about?"

Brandon rubbed the back of his neck, looking uncomfortable.

"What's wrong?"

"He changed the land specs."

"Why would he do that?"

The spot we had picked out was perfect. It wasn't too far off two of the main highways that intersected in town. But it also wasn't too close that the noise would bother the people golfing. And it had a beautiful view of a shallow valley that had a river running through it. A small river, but it was still a pretty sight.

"Where does he want to move it to?"

"He doesn't want to move it. He wants to make it bigger. He wants to build a clubhouse with a tennis court, a swimming pool, and other things. He wants to make it a country club."

"But where is he going to get the rest of the land?" The second the question left my mouth, the answer hit me. "He wants to get rid of the mobile home park, doesn't he?"

Brandon winced. "Notices go out tomorrow that residents need to find somewhere else to live. They have sixty days."

"Why? Why would he do this?" A lightbulb went off. *Maddox*. I swore. "I have to go. I'll walk you out."

Brandon looked confused at my statement. "Okay."

"Where are you staying?"

"At the motel for now."

Our little town had only one place for out-of-town guests to stay.

"Okay. I might need you for something else."

"Whatever you need. I know you care about the people in this town, and I knew you would be upset by this."

I put my hand on Brandon's arm when we got to the door. "Thank you for warning me."

We each got in our cars and drove away from my father's house. I immediately picked up my phone and called Maddox.

No answer.

"*Damn it.*"

I just *knew* in my gut that my father was doing this because Maddox was back in town, and his mother lived in the trailer park. All that talk at dinner, pretending like I wasn't part of the golf course project, was bullshit. My father had known it was my idea from the beginning, and he knew it could come back to me when Maddox found out his mother was going to lose her home.

I had never seen my father stoop so low.

I was furious. I almost turned around to yell at him, but two things stopped me. His health. I didn't want him to have another stroke on me. And I needed to find Maddox.

Something had changed that day in the garage. After our almost-violent screwing, he'd been tender. I felt as if he'd opened up a part of himself he'd been holding back. And he'd been coming to me every night since. He still left before dawn, but sometimes, he would stay and hold me after we had sex.

I feared that, if Maddox found out about his mom from anyone but me, he'd think I was behind it. I needed to talk to him as soon as possible.

I called him once more. Again, there was no answer.

When I got home, Maddox's SUV was parked in the back, but when I ran upstairs to his apartment and knocked, no one was there.

I tried to calm myself. I would just tell Maddox when he got home and came over that night. It would be okay. But, just in case, I sent him a text as I walked back home.

Before I went to bed, I cracked my window up a bit, so I would hear him when he came home. And, while I waited, I planned on how I could fix this problem that my father had created. If he thought I would just sit back, he was wrong.

An hour or so later, I drifted off to sleep, knowing what I had to do the next day.

When I woke up in the morning, I was ready to take on the day.

Unfortunately, five seconds after I woke, I realized that Maddox had never come home.

24

MADDOX

I woke up, feeling the most refreshed I'd felt in a long-ass time. I rolled over and realized I was sleeping in my old bedroom at my mom's. I looked at my watch. It was after ten in the morning.

I had lain down after dinner last night, planning to just take a nap, but I had slept all night. It was true that I was due for some good sleep. Fucking my ex-girlfriend every night and constantly getting up to leave early had really cut into my sleep schedule. But I was still shocked to see I had slept over twelve hours.

I used the bathroom and went into the kitchen in search of some coffee. On my way, I picked up my phone in the living room. It was dead.

"Mom?"

"Yes?"

"Can I borrow your phone charger?"

"Sure. It's in here," my mom said from the kitchen.

"Oh, thank God," I said when I walked in. "Coffee." I

plugged my cell in and grabbed a cup. "Why didn't you wake me?" I asked.

My mom grabbed my chin in her hand. "Because you looked so peaceful, sleeping. I didn't have the heart. You were even snoring."

I shook her off. "Liar."

She laughed. "But you were sleeping hard. Are you not getting any sleep at your new place?"

I took a sip of my coffee. "I am." Just not as much as I should be.

She patted my chest. "I'm worried about you."

I laughed. If she only knew. "Don't be, Mom. I'm fine. I just need to go to bed earlier."

"If you're sure."

"Yes." She was the one who was sick. Not me. "You don't need to worry."

"It's what mothers do."

There was a knock at the door.

I frowned. "Are you expecting anyone?"

"No."

I went to the front door and looked out the window before opening it. I didn't recognize the guy.

"Open the door, Maddox."

"I don't know who it is."

"For heaven's sake, this is Brook Creek. You lived in the big city for too long."

I rolled my eyes, but she did have a point, so I opened the door.

A stranger was wearing a suit and held an envelope in his hand. "Good morning. I'm looking for Betty Wolfe."

My mother pushed in front of me. "I'm Betty."

The man handed her the envelope. "This is for you. If

you have any questions, you can call the number at the bottom." The man turned and left without another word.

I closed the door, and my mom opened the envelope and pulled out a letter.

As I watched her read it, all the color drained from her face, and she grabbed the couch behind her.

"Oh, dear. What am I going to do?"

What the fuck?

I steadied my mom, and then I snatched the letter from her hand. As I read it, a slow anger settled over me. I crumbled up the paper and threw it across the room.

I'm going to kill her.

I marched to the kitchen and turned on my phone.

My mom raced after me. "What are you doing?"

"Looking for the person responsible for this. And then I'm going to wring her pretty little neck."

It looked like I'd missed several phone calls before my phone died. They were all from Addison. She'd also sent me a text message.

I pulled up her number and hit Send.

"Who are you calling?"

"Addison."

The phone went to voice mail.

"She was here this morning. While you were sleeping."

I hit End on my phone and looked up at my mom. "What?"

"She was here this morning."

I pointed to the floor. "Here? As in this house?"

"Yes," my mother said like I was stupid.

"What did she want?"

"A dollar."

What?

"A dollar?" That didn't make any sense. "Did she say why?"

"She said she would explain later and that she didn't have time because she needed to stop at every trailer in the park."

What the hell is that woman up to now?

"I don't know what I'm going to do, Maddox. Where will I go? I can't afford to move my house to another park."

I grabbed my mom's upper arms. "Mom, I'm not going to let them kick you out of here."

"Maddox, I don't own this land. I just pay the lot fee."

"I know." I knew exactly who owned the land. That fucker Brantley Graham.

I kissed my mother on the forehead. "I'm going to get to the bottom of this, okay? We're not going down without a fight."

I pushed my feet into my boots and headed to Addison's office.

I had walked over to my mom's the afternoon before for the exercise, but now, I was regretting it. I didn't have the patience that it was going to take me to walk to her office. I wanted to get there now, so I could yell at her for being such an insensitive bitch.

I tried calling her again, but this time, I went straight to voice mail.

"Fuck."

I thought she was ignoring me.

I picked up the pace and ran almost the whole way. When I got there, I was starting to sweat, but I didn't care. I pulled open the door, and Serena looked up.

"Hey, Uncle Maddox." She wrinkled her nose. "You look like you could use a shower."

"Thanks," I said, ignoring her jab. "Is Addison here?"

"No, she said she was going to be gone all day. Do you want me to take a message?"

"So, you don't know when she'll be back?"

Serena shook her head. "No, but she said she would call before she was on her way home. I can let you know when that is."

I nodded once. "Please do. I need to talk to her." I turned to leave but paused. "Oh, and, Serena?"

"Yeah?"

"Don't tell her I was looking for her, okay?"

"Okay," she said warily.

"Thanks," I said and headed out the door.

25

ADDISON

I trudged to my car, feeling defeated.

I'd driven to Iowa City early that morning to speak to the CEO and board of directors of Brandon's company to try to reason with them. I knew there was no point in trying to convince my father to change his mind, so I'd hoped to appeal to the company's compassion.

I'd lost. The board had agreed to help a little, but in the end, the mobile home park was going. Not only were they afraid my father would change his mind about the project, but they also liked his idea of turning it into a full country club. It would only bring in more revenue, and some of the added features would help offset the money they would lose in the winter when it was too cold, and there was too much snow to golf.

I had to hand it to my dad. He was one smart man. Ruthless and cunning but smart.

I pretty much drove home on autopilot, using the hour-long drive to try to figure out what I was going to do next. It was hard because I really needed to sit down at my computer and do some digging and research.

When I got back to Brook Creek, I parked in my usual spot and walked into the office through the back door.

Serena looked surprised to see me. "Oh, you're back. I thought you were going to call."

"Yeah, sorry. I was preoccupied. Did I miss anything?"

"Just that Uncle Maddox was looking for you." She put a hand up by her mouth. "Don't tell him I said that."

I pulled my phone out of my purse and looked at my blank screen. I'd forgotten to turn it back on. I pushed the power button now.

I'd gotten a phone call in the waiting room, and I hadn't bothered to see who it was. I'd just turned it off completely, so there wouldn't be any distractions.

After my cell powered up, I saw that it was Maddox who'd called me.

Crap.

I'd wanted to talk to him, but now, I felt so drained. There was only one thing I wanted to do. And it wasn't to talk to anyone. Even research was going to have to wait.

"I'll be in my office," was all I said to Serena.

I threw my purse on my desk and went to the corner of the room where my file cabinet was stored.

I sat on the floor, opened the bottom drawer, and reached into the back.

Jackpot.

I pulled my consolation prize out of the back and hugged the package to my chest.

I tried to stay away from chocolate because, once I started eating it, I found it difficult to stop. But, damn it, I deserved some food medication right now.

I unwrapped my bite-sized Reese's Peanut Butter Cup and popped it into my mouth. It didn't really make me feel any better, but it sure as shit tasted damn good.

I lay back on the floor and unwrapped another.

A short time later, I heard the bell ding as the front door opened.

"Where is she?" a deep voice said.

"In her office," Serena said.

I closed my eyes. I didn't want to face Maddox right now.

I heard the heavy tread of his boots as he entered my room.

"What the hell are you doing?"

I opened my eyes. "Feeling sorry for myself."

"You're feeling sorry for yourself? You really are selfish, Addison Graham."

I'd never seen such anger in his eyes, and it was directed at me.

I burst into tears.

I was on the birth control shot, so I didn't get my period, but I still went through my cycle, emotions and food cravings and all. I was pretty sure that was why I was drowning myself in chocolate and why I was crying. My stressful day had come at the wrong time of the month.

"Whoa, whoa, whoa," Maddox said, his face softening as he got down on his haunches.

Like most men, he looked uncomfortable around a weeping woman.

"I'm sorry, Maddox. I tried. I really did. But they won't back down."

He shook his head. "I don't know what you're talking about." He held out his hand. "Here, let me help you up."

I put my hand in his, and he pulled me into a sitting position. The crinkle of wrappers falling off my chest sounded as they landed in my lap.

Maddox picked one up and raised an eyebrow.

"Chocolate therapy," I explained.

He wiped a tear off my face. "It doesn't look like it's working."

I hiccuped, and new tears started to flow. "It's not."

Maddox shook his head. "I really want to be mad at you, but you're making it very hard to do."

"I'm-I'm sorry. I'd be mad at me, too. I'm guessing your mom got the notice that she needs to move?"

His mouth flattened into a grim line. "Yes."

"This is all my fault." I unwrapped another peanut butter cup and shoved it in my mouth. "But I swear, this wasn't part of the original plans," I said over my mouthful of chocolate.

He tilted his head. "It wasn't?"

"No." I frowned. "I would never do that." *Does he really think so little of me?* "I went to Iowa City this morning to talk them out of it. I was even prepared to threaten them with a class action lawsuit, but let's face it. I don't have the funds to take them on."

A look of understanding crossed his face. "Is that why you asked my mom for a dollar this morning?"

I sniffled. "Yes. It was my retainer fee, so I could represent everyone in the trailer park."

"Did you get a dollar from everyone?"

I wiped my cheek. "Almost. Enough that I could legally represent them."

"You really care about the people you represent, don't you?"

Didn't he ask me a similar question like that the other day?

"Yes. I never wanted anything like this to happen."

"So, what did happen?"

"My father."

Maddox swore.

"I know. He's gone too far this time."

"Why would he do this?"

I didn't want to tell Maddox my theory. It sounded so silly to say it out loud to him. I wasn't his girlfriend. We weren't in love. I didn't want him to tell me my father's plan was ridiculous because we weren't even together. I was already too emotional, and as much as I hated to admit it, Maddox meant too much to me. Try as I might to keep him at arm's length, he was becoming too important to me.

But it was obvious that he didn't feel the same, so I shrugged. "I don't know. Money, I guess."

"It's always money."

Usually. Not always.

I looked up at his green eyes, and I felt my eyes began to get wet again. "I'm sorry."

I didn't know if I'd said sorry for the mobile home park/golf course mess or because I was starting to cry again.

"Do you need to do anything else around the office today?"

I held up my bag of candy. "Just finish this off."

Maddox took the chocolate out of my hand and set it on the filing cabinet. "Come on, baby." He put his arms underneath my back and legs and picked me up. "I know something better than drowning yourself in sweets."

26

MADDOX

I carried Addison upstairs to her apartment, yelling at Serena first to let her know that Addison was done for the day and to lock up before she went home.

I took Addison to her bathroom and set her on her feet. I turned on the water in the shower and then proceeded to undress her.

"What are you doing?"

"Sometimes, the best way to get rid of a bad day is to wash it away."

"Does it work?" she asked as she took off her top and bra.

"Sometimes."

I finished undressing her and then took off my own clothes. I ran my finger over the bite mark I'd left on her the other day. I guided both of us under the spray and then slowly washed Addison's day away.

I had shown up at her office, fully ready to yell at her, and she'd completely caught me off guard when she started crying. I'd dated enough women to know when they were fake tears and real ones, and I knew that Addison was sincerely distraught.

The fact that she'd gone to take on a company by herself with only forty dollars as retainers showed me how dedicated she was. I believed her when she'd said she didn't want my mother to lose her home.

When the soap and shampoo was all washed away, I turned off the water and grabbed us some towels from the shelf in the bathroom. I dried us off and took Addison to her bedroom.

"Throw on something comfortable," I told her.

"Is this code for *put on something sexy*?"

I laughed. "No. I mean it. Put on sweats or whatever it is women wear when they want to veg out."

"Yoga pants."

"Yoga pants?"

"Yeah. The most comfortable pair of pants."

I smiled. "Okay then. Put on some yoga pants."

I left her to get dressed and went back to the bathroom to put my clothes back on. I could go home and find new clothes, but I had showered only a few hours before Addison got home.

After I hadn't been able to get ahold of her that morning, I'd called Foster to tell him I wasn't coming in, and I had gone and worked out instead. I'd worked myself so hard; I'd had no choice but to shower before I scared people away with my smell.

I met Addison back in the living room and guided her to the couch. "So, tell me what happened today."

She looked at me and pouted. "When you said you had better therapy than food, I thought you meant sex. I want my chocolate back."

I laughed and pulled her into my arms. "Maybe later. If you're good. But, right now, you need to talk and then relax a little. Tell me about today."

"I went to Iowa City to talk to the company in charge of building the golf course. They won't back down. I did get them to agree to rebuild the park in a new location and move everyone's trailers for free."

The rush of relief went through me. "That's good news, right?"

"Yeah, except I don't know where we're going to move it to. I don't know of any land for sale. And, anything my father owns, I know he's going to say no."

"But he's going to lose all the lot rent he charges the park residents now. Are you sure he'll say no?"

"Not one hundred percent, but I'm pretty sure. And, whatever he loses in lot rent, he'll more than make up for in the golf course. Rather than selling the land outright, he's giving them the land for a nice chunk of shares."

"Well, fuck."

She laughed. "Yeah, that pretty much sums it up."

I squeezed her tight. "Don't admit defeat yet. We'll find someplace to move the park to. The fact that you got them to agree to that is amazing in itself."

She lifted a shoulder. "I guess."

I kissed her on her forehead. "No, *I guess* about it. I'm sorry I called you selfish earlier."

"It's okay. You were mad."

"No, it's not okay. You are incredible. You should be proud of yourself for what you accomplished today."

She didn't say anything, and I didn't press the issue.

I ordered us pizza from the local gas station in town because we didn't have an actual pizzeria, picked it up, and brought it back to her place, figuring there was no better food therapy than pepperoni and mozzarella cheese.

After we finished eating and the leftovers were put away, Addison fell asleep on the couch. I was debating on whether or not I should carry her to bed when there was a knock at her door.

I looked at my watch. It was a little after eight. Not terribly late, but I did wonder who was making a house call at that time.

I opened the door to see a good-looking man standing on the other side. I had several inches and about twenty pounds of muscles on him, but I could tell the guy was fit.

"I'm sorry. I was looking for Addison. I thought she lived above her office."

I blocked the doorway with my body and crossed my arms. "Who's asking?"

His brow furrowed. "I'm sorry. Does Addison live here or not?"

"She does, but she's sleeping right now."

Two small hands touched my sides. "Stand down, Maddox."

I reluctantly stepped to the side.

Addison rubbed the sleep from one of her eyes and pulled down her T-shirt. I didn't like that because it was obvious she wasn't wearing a bra.

"Hey, Brandon. What's up?"

"Do you mind if I come in?"

Hell no.

"Sure," she said, stepping aside to let him in.

Brandon made sure not to get too close to me as he walked into the apartment. Addison sat back down on the couch, but I kept my place at the door.

"You're welcome to sit down," Addison said to Brandon.

He looked warily at me. "No, thanks."

Yeah, man. Don't be getting ideas about my woman.

Addison rolled her eyes. "Maddox, this is Brandon, my ex-boyfriend."

I narrowed my eyes. If she thought pointing out that they no longer dated made things better, it didn't. I didn't like the idea of this putz's hands on her, in the past or otherwise.

"Brandon works for the company that is developing the golf course. He's the one overseeing the project," Addison explained to me.

"So, it's your fault that my mother is going to lose her home."

Brandon visibly paled.

That's right. Be afraid. I've been trained to kill people.

"He's also the one who warned me about your mother losing her home," she said to me. "So, relax. He's on our side." She looked at her ex. "And, Brandon, this is Maddox. He looks scarier than he is."

Brandon's eyes lit up with acknowledgment. "This isn't *the* Maddox, is it?" he asked Addison.

"My ex-boyfriend from high school? Yes."

I growled deep in my throat. So low that neither of them heard the primal response in me.

I didn't like her calling me her ex-boyfriend. Brandon, yes. Me, no.

27

ADDISON

I filled Brandon in on what had happened at his place of employment that day, and he promised to help me find new land.

The whole time we talked, Maddox sat in the corner and scowled. I sensed he didn't like Brandon being there, but I didn't blame Maddox. I wouldn't be too keen on a guy I'd just met, knowing he worked for the company that was forcing my mother to find a new place to live.

I walked Brandon to the door while Maddox was in the bathroom.

"Are you okay with him?" Brandon nodded to the bathroom.

"Yeah."

He didn't look convinced. "I thought he was in prison."

Because I had dated Brandon for so long, he knew a lot about my past with Maddox. And, since we were still friends, he was naturally curious.

I sighed. "It's a long story. I'll fill you in sometime."

"Okay. Call me if you need anything."

"I will."

I shut the door behind Brandon. Then, I went and turned off the television. I went to my room to lie down on my bed. The sun was on its way down, and I was tired. Maddox knew where to find me to say good-bye. I closed my eyes while I waited for him.

I awoke sometime later. It was completely dark outside, except for the lights coming from the alley through the window.

I heard a rustling off to the side and saw Maddox walk into my room. He put both hands at the bottom of his shirt and pulled it over his head. Then, he unbuttoned his pants and pushed them to the floor along with his boxers.

He took the two steps to my bed, looking magnificent and extremely hard.

"You're still here," I stated the obvious because, apparently, I didn't know what else to say in the face of such masculinity.

"Yeah." He leaned over, grabbed my yoga pants by the waist, and pulled them off.

"What have you been doing?"

"Thinking." He grasped my hand. "Sit up."

"What were you thinking about?"

He hauled me to a sitting position and stripped my shirt off. "You. Me." He met my eyes. "Us."

"And what did you decide?" I was almost afraid to ask.

"That I want you on your knees."

It wasn't the answer I had been looking for, but I grew wet from his words. I slid off the bed and onto the floor in front of him.

"Put my cock in your mouth, Addison."

I didn't know why I had waited for directions. I loved giving him head. There was something extra special about showing the guy who had taught you to give blow jobs how much you'd perfected your skills.

I took ahold of his shaft and lifted it up, so I could suck his sack into my mouth. Maddox moaned. That one I'd learned on my own. Men liked more than just their dicks to be sucked.

I moved my mouth to his cock and pushed him past my lips, twirling my tongue around the head as I did so. When he hit a certain spot, I concentrated on flattening my tongue and sucking him as far as I could go. I gagged on his length and girth a few times, but I took him all the way, my nose touching his stomach.

I pulled my mouth away, so I could breathe better, spit hanging off both of us. I didn't care. It meant I was sucking him off right.

Maddox wrapped a hand around the front of my throat. It didn't hurt, and I wasn't scared. It was a possessive move and made my pussy ache.

"I'm going to fuck your mouth like that again. But, when I tell you to, I want you to suck on the head. I'm going to come in your mouth, and I want my seed to hit your tongue. I want you to taste me. I want you to know it's me coming down your throat."

I moaned as I took him back in my mouth. My jaw was going to be sore tomorrow, but it was going to be worth it. When it was time for him to come, he tapped on my head, but I didn't need the signal. I still knew his body well enough. His cock had started to swell, and his pre-cum had gotten thicker. I knew he was ready.

I wrapped my lips around his tip as Maddox knocked my hands away. It took some effort to only use my mouth, but I kept him where we both wanted him as he came. His flavor hit my tongue, and I swallowed him down.

He grabbed on to his cock and squeezed, pushing the last bit of cum into my mouth before he pulled away from me.

He was breathing hard, and he rubbed a thumb over my lips. "This mouth is mine." He stepped back and lifted his chin toward my bed. "Up on the bed. On your back."

I scrambled up, excited to see what would happen next.

Maddox pulled me to the edge, and this time, he got down on his knees. He pushed a finger inside me and pulled it out. He held it up, so the light glistened off it. "Always so wet." He put his finger into his mouth and sucked it off.

He gripped my hips in a tight grasp and spread my thighs wide as he buried his face between my legs. His tongue attacked my clit, and since I was already turned on, I knew it wouldn't take me long. But Maddox went from sucking to running his tongue around it.

I tried to rotate my hips against his face.

He smacked the side of my ass. "Behave. I'll tell you when you can fuck my face."

God, I loved being bossed around.

After a few licks of my cleft and a little more teasing from his tongue, he flicked my clit again, and I exploded. He held on to my thighs and continued to lick me until I begged him to stop. He let my legs go, and they flopped open because my limbs had lost the ability to move.

I touched his smooth chest as he shifted my hips, so our

bodies were on the bed the long way now. He was hard again, and I watched him push into me.

"Oh God," I moaned. I was swollen and sensitive from my orgasm, and I felt every inch of him.

Maddox fell over me and kissed each of my breasts as he slowly thrust inside me. His mouth moved up my body until it was on mine.

I flung my arms around his neck and kissed him. I loved the way Maddox kissed, and I hadn't realized how much I had missed it until the day at the auto garage. He made love to my mouth as his body made love to mine.

Soon, our breathing picked up, and I knew I was close to another climax.

"I'm going to come inside your pussy, and I want you to come with me."

"I'll try."

He smiled and kissed me. "You will."

He pushed my one leg higher and began to drive his cock into me with strong, precise moves. The head of his cock repeatedly hit my G-spot, and I understood why he was so confident that I would come when he did.

I felt the beginning tingles, telling me I was close.

"That's it, baby. Come for me."

His words took me over, and my eyes closed with the force of my orgasm. I cried out at the intensity of it as I heard Maddox grunt, and his warm seed flooded my insides.

I was now a puddle of jelly, but I managed to open my eyes as I watched Maddox slowly pull his cock from my body. He sat back on his heels and stared at my pussy.

He rubbed his thumb over it from bottom to top.

I shivered when he brushed my clit.

"My pussy," he said. He looked up at me again. "Are you okay?"

"Yes."

"Good. Because we're not done yet."

28

MADDOX

Addison's eyes grew wide at this statement, but she didn't protest.

I got up from her bed and went to her bathroom. I searched through her medicine cabinet and drawers. Nothing fit what I was looking for.

Next, I went to the kitchen and attacked her cupboards. Above the stove, I found exactly what I wanted.

I carried my find back to the bedroom and set it on the nightstand. I lay down next to Addison. Her dark hair was a mess. She looked like she'd been thoroughly fucked.

She raised her eyebrows. "What's with the coconut oil?"

"Do you trust me?"

"Uh…"

I pushed her onto her back and sucked a nipple in my mouth. She moaned and squirmed under me. I made a mental note to come all over her pretty tits sometime soon.

I released her reddened tip. "It's a simple question, Addy. Do you trust me?" I flicked the opposite nipple between my teeth and tongue.

"Yes," she said, her voice almost breathless.

Music to my ears.

I released her breast and looked down at her. "Good."

I pushed two fingers into her pussy and caressed her G-spot. She was already wet from her earlier orgasms and me coming inside her. I pulled my hand away and painted both her nipples with our cum. That would have to do for now.

I pushed my digits back into her, this time using my thumb to stroke her clit, too. She bucked underneath my hand.

"Are you going to come again?"

"Yes."

"When?"

"Soon."

I stopped rubbing. "Not yet."

She whimpered in protest.

I leaned over and kissed her. I pushed my tongue past her lips, and she greedily sucked on it.

I nipped her bottom lip and lifted my head. "I promise, I won't let you suffer. You'll get your orgasm."

"You're such a tease."

I grinned. I slowly pulled my fingers from her pussy, dragging her wetness to her tight little hole in her rear.

Not knowing if she'd ever done this before, I only pressed one finger into her.

Her eyes widened with surprise, but then I felt her body relax.

"Have you done this before?"

"Yes."

"Have you ever been fucked here?"

"Yes."

I could admit, I was a little disappointed that I wouldn't

be her first, but I guessed I had already taken her mouth and pussy virginity. I couldn't be too greedy.

I added another finger, and she winced.

"It's been a few years," she explained.

This news made me smile inside.

I took my hand away and rolled to grab the coconut oil from the nightstand. I unscrewed the cover and scooped out a generous amount, coating my fingers and grabbing a little extra.

I lifted my leg, so my knee was slightly bent. "Put your leg over mine."

I thought about having her bend over, but I wanted to watch her as I took her ass for the first time.

She rested her leg on top of mine, opening her up more for my assessment.

I spread the oil on her backside before sliding a finger inside her again. "Touch your clit," I commanded as I pushed in a second digit, which slipped in a lot easier now that she was lubed up.

I lost my train of thought for a moment as I watched her touch herself. Addison did not shy away from masturbation because it looked to me like she knew exactly what to do to make herself feel good.

When I felt she was ready, I pushed in a third finger, and she moaned.

"Somebody likes getting her ass fucked."

She bit her lip and smiled. "Maybe."

I was able to get my fingers in to the third knuckle with little resistance, and I figured it was time.

I grabbed the jar of coconut oil and took enough out to coat my dick. Then, I took her hand from her pussy and sucked on her fingers. "I'll be the only one touching you there now."

She gave me an *oh really* look, and I laughed.

"Are you ready?"

"Yes."

I rubbed my cock on the rim of her asshole. "Has Brandon ever fucked you like this?"

"No."

"Good," I said and pushed into her.

She grabbed on to my shoulders. "Fuck, Maddox."

"You okay?"

"Yes, you're just so big."

"Woman, you say that like it's a bad thing." I kissed her mouth. "Relax. Let me fuck you good."

I brushed my thumb over her clit as I started to thrust. My movements started out gently. It was only after she was moaning and rubbing her ass all over my dick that I really started to pound her, but I couldn't quite do what I wanted in that position.

I pulled out and slapped her ass. "On your knees."

She quickly did as I'd asked, and I got behind her. Her ass puckered like it wanted my cock again, and who was I to say no? I clutched her shoulders as I drove into her.

God, her ass was nice and tight and felt almost as good as her pussy.

I reached under her and caressed her clit as I pounded her from behind.

Addison's cries were getting louder and more frequent as she squeezed her asshole around my dick.

As this would be my third orgasm of the night, I was shocked when I felt the tightening of my nuts and the tingling at the bottom of my spine.

I should have known Addison would be the one to get me to come again without any troubles.

Right as her orgasm broke, I slammed inside her one last time and emptied my balls into her.

I pulled out and brushed my thumb over her rear channel, spreading my cum around it. “Mine.”

29

ADDISON

A twinge in my backside woke me from my slumber. I stilled my body and willed myself to go back to sleep, but I could tell it wasn't going to happen. I blinked my eyes and looked at my alarm clock. It was just after five a.m.

Ugh. Why the hell am I up so early?

Oh, yeah, I'd taken a nap on the couch and gone to bed at about eight last night. Of course I was awake.

That, and my sore ass.

Not that I was complaining.

Much.

I'd had a pretty magnificent orgasm out of it. And the fact that it was number three was saying something. Usually, orgasm number one topped all the others.

I had no idea what had come over Maddox last night, but I had liked it. His alpha male—*me caveman, you mine* thing—was hot. Then, when I'd turned on the fan and told him I was going to shower, he'd pulled me back to the bed and told me I wasn't allowed to wash his seed from me.

I rolled onto my back and looked at the empty spot beside me. Too bad I'd had to wake up alone again.

I should be used to it by now, but I wasn't.

I was truly disappointed that I was alone, so when my half-closed door was pushed open, I about peed the bed.

Maddox walked in, naked, beautiful, and sporting a very nice erection.

"What are you doing?" I croaked since it was the first thing I'd said since waking.

He rubbed his face and got under the covers. "Going back to sleep. I'm still tired." He closed his eyes and put a pillow over his face.

I got up on my elbows. "Where were you?"

"Bathroom," he said from behind the big bulk of cotton.

"Doing what?"

"Taking a piss."

Huh. Color me surprised. "So, you've been here all night?"

"Jesus, Addison, will you be quiet? I'm going to have a long day at work. I have to make up for not being there yesterday. I just want to go back to sleep."

I wrinkled my nose. "You're a crab. Do you always wake up this grouchy?"

He whipped the pillow off his head and yanked me under him. He narrowed his eyes at me. "If you don't shut up, I'm going to fuck you into silence."

I didn't say a word.

His body relaxed.

But, right before he rolled off of me, I said, "I don't think you can technically fuck someone into silence. As you know, I'm quite vocal when we—"

Maddox pushed into me with one smooth move.

"*Holy shit.*"

"You're right. You scream way too much when I'm inside you. But I'm going to fuck you anyway."

I tiptoed out of my bedroom, so I wouldn't wake Maddox. It was true; I liked the morning sex, but he really was grumpy, so I thought I should let him sleep.

First thing on my agenda was to make coffee. As I filled up the tank and put in the scoops, I realized that I had no idea if Maddox drank coffee or not. He hadn't back in high school, but a lot could happen in twelve years. I decided it would be better to make extra and throw it away than to not make enough.

As the coffee was brewing, I planned to start up my laptop and do some land research, but my little desk was empty. I had left my computer downstairs.

No biggie. I could just run down and get it. But, as I looked around for my purse where I kept my keys to unlock the office, I remembered that I had thrown it on my desk where it still sat.

Shit.

I went back to the kitchen and opened my horrible mess of a junk drawer. After much rummaging, I found my spare office keys. "Yes."

I ran down, picked up my stuff, relocked the office, and came back upstairs. It was perfect timing because my coffeemaker beeped just as I opened the door.

I poured myself a cup and sat down at my desk.

After my computer started, I pulled up a map of our town. If I looked at it like a square, on one side would be the new golf course, and on another side was the only motel and the county line, so expanding that way wasn't a good idea. So, that left the north side of town and the east.

Ideally, the east side would be best because it would put downtown, the grocery store, and the two restaurants in about the same amount of distance.

An hour or so later, I was feeling excited because I had an idea. I was so engrossed in my research; I didn't notice Maddox was awake until he wrapped his arm around my shoulders. He pushed my hair off my shoulder and kissed my neck.

"What are you doing?"

"Trying to find a way to save the mobile home park. I think I have a plan."

When Maddox didn't say anything, I looked over at him.

He was grinning.

"What?" I asked.

He shook his head. "Nothing, babe." He nodded to my coffee cup. "You have any of that for me?"

"In the kitchen."

He kissed my neck again and went into the kitchen. He returned a minute later. He was only wearing his jeans, and I got lost in his bare torso.

How could I have so much sex with a man and still be mesmerized by his nakedness?

He might have said something, but I didn't really hear him because the blood had left my head and traveled south.

"Hey, Addy?"

"Huh?" I looked up to his face.

He smirked. "Baby, what did you find out?"

"About what?"

He laughed and shook his head. He walked over to me

and crouched down. "You know I feel the same way about you, right?"

"Huh?"

He ran his finger over the spot where he'd bitten me when we had sex in the auto garage. At the time, I'd been too overcome with ecstasy to notice he broke the skin. Later, it had hurt, but I kind of liked that he'd marked me. Today, it was nearly healed, and I barely felt it anymore.

"Last night, while you were taking your little nap, I decided to stop fighting this. The past is in the past. Forgive and forget, you know."

"Huh?" I had no idea what he was getting at.

He dropped his head and shook it. When he looked up at me again, his eyes were sparkling with laughter. "Is that all you can say? *Huh*?"

"No."

"Good, because we have some talking to do. But, first, tell me what you think we can do to save my mother's home."

30

MADDOX

I watched Addison as she hung up the phone with Brandon and threw it on the couch.

She looked at me and smiled. "He said that he's meeting with the architect this morning, but then he's free this afternoon. He also said he needs to talk to his boss just to make sure he knows how much money he can offer." She rubbed her hands together. "I have a good feeling about this."

Even though I didn't want her meeting with her ex-boyfriend and hanging out with him, I had a good feeling, too.

I pulled her into my arms and cupped the back of her neck. I then proceeded to kiss the hell out of her. When I separated our lips, I said, "Keep me updated. I gotta go get ready for work." Setting her on her feet, I let her go. "I'll talk to you later." With a slap on her ass, I was out of there.

I went to my apartment, threw on work clothes, grabbed my keys, and took off for the garage.

When I walked into the back, my brother came out of the office and scowled at me. "A word, please?"

I followed him back into the office. "What's up?"

"Where have you been?"

I didn't really see how that was any of Foster's business. I crossed my arms over my chest. "Around."

"You were with Addison, weren't you? You were supposed to go and *talk* to her. Our mom is going to lose her home because of that bitch, and you're busy fucking her."

I wrapped my hand around my brother's throat and slammed him against the wall. "You don't ever talk about her like that again."

Foster shook me off. "You need to get your head on straight. Look what happened to you the last time you got involved with her."

"First of all, if you hadn't dressed up as me and broken the fucking law, she wouldn't have had to be my alibi in the first place."

My brother flinched, and I watched guilt cloud his face.

"Second, that bitch, as you called her, has been working her ass off the last twenty-four hours to fix this mess. She didn't ask for this, and she didn't want it."

Foster sneered. "You're fucking pussy-whipped."

I clenched my fists and released them. "So help me, God. Foster, I am trying not to punch the shit out of you right now." I sighed. "This was her father's doing. This was not her decision, and it's not something she wants."

"It's still her fault. Serena told me all about how it was her idea that brought this whole golf course shit to our doorsteps."

"You're an unforgiving bastard, you know that? You would think that, as someone who fucked up and made mistakes, you'd have a little more understanding."

I could tell he wasn't going to let this go, but his voice did soften as he said, "I just don't want to see you get hurt again."

"Are you planning on robbing any more gas stations?"

"Fuck you," Foster said and stomped out of the office.

"Yeah, fuck you, too, asshole," I yelled after him.

After our fight, I started working on an old Chevy, hoping it would take my mind off things. At lunchtime, my sister stopped in on her break from her job as a bank teller. She brought us both sandwiches, but Foster made an excuse not to eat with us.

"What's his problem?" Kelly asked as we went to sit outside in the break area.

"We kind of got into it this morning."

"About what?" she asked as she unwrapped her sandwich.

I did the same with mine. "Addison."

"Ah..."

I frowned. "What does that mean?"

She laughed. "It means my daughter works with her and heard your conversation in her office. I know she's trying to fix what happened."

"Did you tell Foster that?"

"No. Until now, I haven't seen him since I talked with Serena. He's still pissed?"

"Yes. I tried to tell him that it was her father's fault, but he says she's going to hurt me again."

Kelly took a bite of her sandwich and lifted her brow.

I rolled my eyes. "And then I asked him if he planned on knocking over another gas station."

She winced and wiped her mouth with her napkin. "Harsh, dude."

"I know. But he called Addison a bitch. I wasn't feeling very nice."

Kelly tilted her head and studied me. "You're starting to care about her again, aren't you?"

I shrugged.

"I thought men were supposed to separate sex and love?"

"Ha-ha." With other women, yes. With Addison, it was complicated. "I've just seen a different side of her since I came back to town. She really cares about her clients and the people of Brook Creek. I don't know what happened twelve years ago, but I would like to think she had a good reason for not alibiing me."

Kelly skeptically looked at me. "I agree that she's not as heartless as we originally thought, but I don't know. She'd have to be lying on her death bed if it were me doing the forgiving."

"Yeah, well…" That was probably why I hadn't asked her about it yet. I didn't want reality to ruin the little fantasy I had going on in my head. "Right now, we're just enjoying each other."

"You know, you're going to have to talk to her eventually."

"Yes, Mom, thank you for the advice," I said mockingly.

She stuck her tongue out at me.

"So, what's Addison's plan?" Kelly asked a few minutes later.

"We're going to try to get the park moved. She worked out some deal with the company that's building the golf course."

Her eyebrows went up again. "We?"

"Yes, we. I told her I'd help however I could."

"You got it bad, dude."

"Stop saying dude. It sounds weird."

"Okay, dude. Whatever you say, dude."

"You're such a brat. Aren't you my older sister?"

"Yeah, dude, I am, dude."

"I think I'd rather be hanging out with Foster," I said under my breath.

Kelly just laughed.

31

ADDISON

I waved at Brandon as I walked into the diner. He was already seated in one of the booths, and I slid in on the opposite side to join him.

"So, what are you thinking?" he asked me.

"Well, I have no idea if this will work, but a couple of years back, Dan Davis put a big chunk of his farmland up for sale. He sold some of it to his neighbor but not as much as he wanted. He still has over sixty acres, and I thought maybe he'd be willing to sell your company several of those acres for the mobile home park."

"Have you talked to him yet?"

I smiled uncomfortably. "I was kind of hoping you'd go with me. I figured he'd be more likely to say yes if you were there. And, if he had questions, you could answer them." I folded my hands and mouthed, *Please*.

Brandon laughed. "Of course I'll go."

I clapped. "Yay. Thank you."

He grabbed one of the menus that were always kept at

the booths. "Are you sure Maddox is going to be okay with that?"

I frowned. "Yeah. Why wouldn't he be?"

"Seriously? He all but whipped out his dick and pissed a circle around you."

I laughed. "No, he didn't."

Although he had gotten rather possessive after Brandon left, I still thought Brandon was exaggerating by quite a bit.

"So, what's the story with him? What's he doing back?"

I didn't get a chance to answer because Dani came over.

"Hello, I'm Dani, and I'll be helping you today." She grinned at Brandon. She looked at me, her smile not quite as big. "Addison."

Brandon smiled back at her. "I'm Brandon." He studied Dani for a second. "I think we've met before. I came to visit Addison a couple of years ago, and you waited on us."

"Oh, yes." Recognition showed in her eyes, and then she looked confused. "Did you two used to date?" she asked, pointing her pen back and forth between the two of us.

"Yes," Brandon said. "But we're just friends now."

I leaned back in my seat. *Go, Brandon.*

"So, what brings you back to our tiny town?" Dani asked.

"I'm here, overseeing the golf course project."

"Interesting. That means, you'll be here awhile, right?"

Brandon nodded. "A long time."

"So, you'll be here for Brook Days?"

Brandon wrinkled his nose. "Don't you mean Creek Days? I saw signs for it when I was coming into town. And isn't it over?"

"Oh, no," Dani said. "Brook Days is in August, and it's totally separate."

Brandon looked at me.

I shrugged. "It's a small town. We get bored. And we can't cram everything in on one weekend, so they made two. Creek Days, we have the parade and the street dance. Brook Days, we have the chili cook-off and Brook Creek tournament."

"What kind of tournament?"

"There's fishing, baseball, flag football, horseshoes, volleyball...basically anything you can think of," I said.

"So, when is this Brook Days?" Brandon asked Dani.

"The first weekend in August."

"I'll be here." Brandon grinned.

Dani beamed. "Great. Now, what can I get you two to drink?"

After we finished eating, Brandon went to use the restroom, and I got up to pay the bill at the counter.

Dani didn't look at me right away. When she met my eyes, she looked hesitant.

"What?" I asked and smiled. I wanted to reassure her that she could talk to me.

"You and Brandon?"

"Yeah?"

"You're really just friends?"

"Yes."

"Do you mind if I go for him?"

I laughed. "I feel like I'm having déjà vu."

She gave me a look that told me she didn't think I was very funny. "Yeah, well, I tried to go after Maddox, but he turned me down."

This was news to me. "When?" I asked before I realized she might see it as none of my business.

"The night of the street dance."

The night he'd snuck into my room and had sex with me for the first time.

I couldn't help the warm tingle that went through me. He could've had sex with Dani, but he'd picked me.

Dani looked at me with her eyebrows raised, and I realized she was waiting for me to reply.

"Sorry about that."

"Yeah, well, he was always crazy about you. I shouldn't be surprised he didn't take me up on my unspoken offer."

Brandon came out of the restroom at that moment.

I leaned closer. "Brandon and I were nothing like Maddox and me. We really are just friends. Go for it. He's a truly great guy."

Dani grinned. "Great." She handed me the change just as Brandon walked up.

"You ready?"

"Yep."

Brandon waved at Dani. "See ya later."

"Bye."

Once outside, I nudged him with my elbow. "You stud, you."

"Shut up." He was laughing as he said it.

"Do you mind if I drive? I know how to get there."

He held out his arm. "Lead the way."

We walked across the street and then behind the building to my car.

The trip to the farm was short since it was just on the edge of town, but my car was making weird noises.

"What is that?"

Brandon held up his hands. "You're asking the wrong guy. Cars are not my thing."

"Oh, yeah. I forgot that about you."

I pulled out my phone as we drove up the long driveway to the Davis' house.

"Wolfe," his rough voice answered.

"Maddox?"

"Yeah?" his voice said, softer this time.

"Who worked on my car?"

"I don't know. I'd have to look. Why?"

"It's making funny noises. It wasn't making them yesterday." At least I didn't think I'd heard anything. I had been a little preoccupied. "Can I bring it by?"

"I'll come to you. I don't want you driving if something bad is going to happen."

My heart melted a little.

"Where are you?"

"I just got to the Davis farm."

"Okay, I'll see you soon."

32

MADDOX

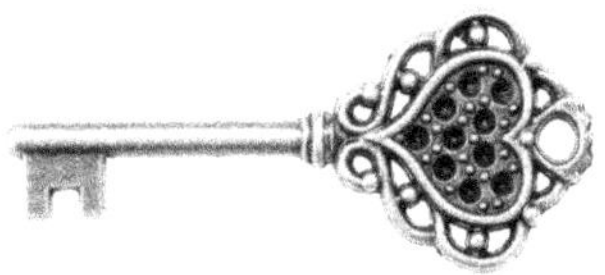

I pulled up to the Davis farm, next to Addison's car, and got out. I'd brought a small toolbox with me, hoping that was all I would need to get her back to the garage.

I opened her car door and heard the ding that warned me the keys were still in the ignition. I had to laugh because, back in Virginia, that would probably get your car stolen. There were some good things about living in small towns.

I turned her engine over but didn't hear anything. I put the car in reverse to see if I could hear anything when driving and realized instantly what Addison's problem was.

I barked out a laugh as I put the car in park and released the parking brake. As I turned the engine off, Addison rushed out of the house. She jumped into my arms the moment I got out of her vehicle.

"What's going on, baby?" I asked as she stepped out of our embrace. I put my arm on the open car door and rested against it.

"He said yes." She moved backward and did a victory dance.

A grin spread across my face. "That's amazing."

"I know. We'll still have more work to do, but we're headed in the right direction." She looked around me and at her car. "Did you figure out what was wrong?"

"Yeah, you had your parking brake on." I held in my laughter this time because I didn't want to make her feel stupid.

Her cheeks turned red anyway. "Oh my God, I'm such an idiot. I ran a couple of errands this morning and parked on a hill." Her eyes widened. "Is this going to cost me money again?"

"You're probably going to need new brakes now since you drove like that for a while."

"Crap."

I leaned closer, wrapping an arm around her and putting my mouth by her ear. "As for the personal service, you can thank me later. But I don't want money." I wanted that sweet, sweet pussy.

She nuzzled my neck. "What are you thinking? A blow job?"

I chuckled. "If you're offering, I'm not going to say no." I dropped my other arm from the car door and ran my finger down the V-neck of her shirt and over the tops of her breasts. "But what I really want to do is come all over your gorgeous tits." There was just something about seeing a woman wearing your cum. "I want to mark them as mine."

I bent my head and took Addison's mouth. I loved how she immediately opened for me and moaned.

The screen door to the house creaked open, and I lifted my head.

Addison stepped to the side of me to see who was coming out, and I dropped my arm from around her.

Brandon came out first with a smile on his face. Dan Davis followed, also smiling, but it fell from his face when he saw me.

"What's he doing here?" Dan pointed to me.

Addison gave me a worried look and walked over to Dan. "Maddox came to look at my car. He's also been helping Brandon and me with the new trailer park idea."

"I rescind my offer."

"Excuse me?" Addison said.

Dan pointed at me. "If that asshole's involved, I'm out."

A look of panic came over Brandon's face. "Sir, please, maybe my company could offer you more money."

"I don't care how much money is involved. You're not from here, son, so I'll explain a few things to you. The Wolfes are bad news. I don't care that his brother and sister have cleaned up their acts because this one"—he pointed to me again—"is the reason my wife's aunt's brother-in-law is dead."

Fuck.

I had totally forgotten the connection between Dan Davis and George Fike. George Fike was the man who'd had a heart attack during my brother's gas station robbery. He was unable to get to the hospital in time and died as a result. It was concluded that he wouldn't have had a heart attack if there hadn't been a robbery, and he wouldn't have died if he hadn't had a heart attack. It had added another charge to robbery crime.

And, while the judge had known I was innocent, the people of this town still blamed me for what had happened. I thought a lot of them had let it go. I'd gotten a few dirty looks here and there, but this was the first outright sign of hate I'd experienced. Of course, I'd been here less than a month.

I wanted to punch Dan Davis for being a selfish asshole. People were going to lose their homes, and he was going to deny them that over a grudge. And, yes, I understood someone had died, but it had been an accident.

But I cared more about my mother than I did my pride, so I bit my tongue and kept my fists to myself.

"I was just leaving," I said. "Please don't let me interfere with anything. I'm sorry for your loss."

I turned to go, meeting Addison's eyes. I could tell she wanted to say something, but I shook my head ever so slightly to tell her no. It wasn't worth it.

She turned and blocked my path. "I'll have you know, sir, that this man is not who you think he is. He's a great person, and we're lucky to have him on the project."

Damn.

If I hadn't already planned to fuck her tonight, I sure was now. Watching her stand up to the old farmer for me was hot as hell.

It was a mistake, but I grinned like a fool.

"He's exactly who I think he is. A lowlife criminal."

Addison stepped away from me, fire in her eyes, and I quickly wrapped my arm around her waist and lifted her off the ground.

She twisted and fought. "Let me go, Maddox. I need to teach the *gentleman* some manners."

I couldn't help but laugh. "Let it go, baby. He's not worth it," I said in her ear.

"And you, young lady, need to learn to keep better company. Everyone knew you were dating this scum back in high school, and they know you're sleeping with him now."

Addison brushed the hair that had fallen over her face out of the way. "I have never denied or hidden that."

"Maybe you should. Everyone's going to think you're a slut for sleeping with him."

"That's it," I said and set Addison down.

The tables had turned, and she put her hands on my chest. I had inches and pounds on her, so her feet slid on the gravel as I moved forward.

"Don't do it, Maddox. He's just trying to rile you up. He wants to show you he's right."

I stopped and looked down at her. "You were ready to go up there and do something to him."

"Yeah, but I'm a female and smaller than him." She grabbed on to my shirt. "Maddox, you're younger and bigger, and you have military training. The sheriff would have a field day with this. Please."

I took a deep breath. "Fine."

She sighed with relief. "Thank you."

"Brandon," I called to the guy.

He'd been standing off to the side, obviously not knowing what to do.

"Yeah?"

"Drive Addison's car back to town, will you? I need to discuss something with her alone."

33

ADDISON

Whatever Maddox had to discuss, it wasn't with me but rather my vagina.

We'd gotten about a mile away from the Davis farm when he pulled over onto a secluded gravel road, opened the tailgate, and commanded I get in the back of his SUV with him. That was where he tugged down my pants and shoved his face between my legs. I didn't even care that the rear door of the SUV was wide open.

I grabbed ahold of his hair and rotated my hips over his face.

Maddox pulled his mouth away and grinned up at me. "You're a greedy little wench, you know that?" He shoved two fingers into me and curled them in a come-hither motion.

"Only for you," I barely managed to say over the pleasure taking over my body.

"Fuck, that's what I like to hear."

Maddox put his head down again, right on my swollen clit. He did this thing where he grazed his teeth over it, almost to the point of biting, but it always felt so good.

I arched my back, telling him with my body that I wanted more. The dual stimulation of my G-spot and clit had me rushing toward release.

But then his mouth and fingers stilled. I wanted to cry.

Maddox lay down beside me. "Come on, gorgeous. I want you to ride me."

It wasn't my favorite position. I was a strong woman and fought for what I believed in, but when it came to the bedroom, I wanted the man to be in control.

"Addison?"

I met Maddox's eyes.

"Get on my fucking cock. Now."

I got up on my knees and straddled him, tucking my chin to my chest and letting my hair fall forward so that he couldn't see my face. I was grinning like a dork. It was like the man knew exactly what I needed.

He grabbed his shaft and swiped it between my nether lips. "Do you want me inside you?"

Always.

"You know I do."

"Good girl." He arched his eyebrows. "Now, slowly slide that sweet pussy down until I'm all the way inside you."

I sank down, gasping at his size when he entered me. You'd think I'd be used to how big he was, especially with how much sex we'd been having, but he still stretched me every time.

When I got him all the way inside me, I had to take a couple of deep breaths.

"Relax, baby."

I smile and nodded.

"Remember just a little while ago how you were ready to feed Davis a piece of your mind?"

"Feed him a piece of my mind? I was ready to scratch his face off."

Maddox laughed. I felt his abs flex under my hands, and his dick pushed just a little further inside me.

I squeaked.

"That's what I love about you. You're ready to go for the jugular."

I sucked in a breath. I knew Maddox hadn't actually said he loved me, but those words had my heart racing.

He didn't even seem to notice what he'd said because he just kept talking, "Now, I want you to take all the anger and those feelings and use it to ride me."

There was one problem with that. "I'm still mad, but I kind of lost the fire I had in that moment."

"So, it doesn't bother you that he called me a lowlife criminal? Or that I'm scum?"

I felt the rage building again. "Of course it bothers me."

"How about that you shouldn't be sleeping with me?"

I leaned down, so our noses touched. "He doesn't know what the fuck he's talking about."

"Show me. Show me I deserve to be inside you," he said in a low voice.

He put his hands on my hips and began to rock me over him.

I wrapped my hands around his head. "Oh, Maddox."

He kissed me, pulling my bottom lip into his mouth and sucking on it, like he'd done with my clit earlier. He released me and licked his way into my mouth.

God, this man tastes good.

And he felt good, too.

His pubic bone was rubbing against my outer sweet spot,

and his cock was almost hitting my inner sweet spot. I just needed to shift my hips a little...

Ah, fuck yeah, right there.

A gasp and then a long moan escaped me.

"Yeah, Addy, keep going. I can tell you're close."

He was right. I was close.

"Come all over me, baby. Come all over me, so I can come inside you." He reached up and thumbed my nipples. "God, I love coming inside you."

That was it. I just needed some of Maddox's filthy talk, and I flew over the edge. I shoved my hips down on him as far as I could and came. I could feel my walls clenching around him, and within seconds, I felt Maddox swell and pump inside me.

I collapsed on his chest, letting my orgasm slowly fade.

Maddox enveloped me in his arms as I felt his cock twitch a few more times. His heart was beating fast under my ear, and it made me smile.

"Remind me to get you mad more often."

I pinched his side. "You'd better not."

He laughed and rubbed his hands up and down my back.

"I don't want to leave." I felt so relaxed and safe in his arms.

"Me either. Except I have to go back to work, and someone could come along and see us."

"Yeah, there is that." I sat up, keeping him inside me. "We're going to be a mess."

"I have some towels in the backseat. I brought them in case I needed to clean up after working on your car."

I raised my fists in the air. "Yay for my parking brake being on," I joked.

Maddox laughed. "Yeah, except my appearance ruined the potential sale."

I cupped his face. "I know you're worried about your mom, but he's not worth it. No one gets to say those things about you. We'll find something else."

He hadn't contacted me in the last twelve years, but I was starting to let that anger go. I saw what a great man he'd become, and I liked having him in my life and in my bed.

Sure, if he ever proposed, I'd have to ask him why he had disappeared without a word. But that wasn't going to happen. At least, not anytime soon. We weren't even officially dating.

Maddox drew me back into his embrace and kissed me.

When he pulled away, he had a look in his eyes that I couldn't figure out. "You're amazing."

I shook my head. "No, you're amazing."

This town didn't deserve him.

He grinned. "How about we agree to disagree?"

I smiled back. "Deal."

34

BRANTLEY

Wednesday afternoon, Brantley Graham looked up from his desk in his office as Simon walked in with a man behind him that Brantley had never met before.

The man stepped forward and held out his hand. "Hello, Mr. Graham. I'm John Spade."

Ah. The PI Brantley hired.

He stood and held out his right hand to welcome the detective. "How do you do?"

"May I sit?"

Brantley swept his arm out. "Please." He looked over at Simon. "Please have a glass of water brought to our guest."

Simon nodded like the good employee he was. Brantley had found the perfect protégé in him. Now, if only he could convince his Addison to marry him.

It was a shame he didn't have a son or a nephew to pass down the business to, but unfortunately, he was an only child, and his Addison was an only child. Her mother had passed away when Addison was six after struggling with cancer for a few years. He had considered remarrying, but he was always too busy, and before he knew it, twenty years had passed.

This was why he needed Addison to stop her foolish fantasies about Maddox Wolfe. That boy would never be worthy of marrying his daughter. It was a godsend that he'd been arrested twelve years ago. Then, his daughter had almost ruined that.

When Sheriff Whitlock had called and told him that she had alibied Maddox, Brantley had been enraged and disgusted. Taking up with a Wolfe. He hit the jackpot though when she was never subpoenaed for Maddox's trial. His court-appointed lawyer had shown up with papers requesting that Addison testify, giving her the ultimate decision to go to court or not.

It was a good thing the paperwork had been "lost" and that he'd had Addison take a trip to visit her mother's parents out of state on the day she was supposed to appear in court.

But, now, the stupid man was back. Back in town. Back in Addison's life. Back in her bed.

Brantley shuddered at the thought as Simon returned to the room.

Behind him, one of the maids came with a glass of water for Mr. Spade.

"Thank you," Mr. Spade said. Then, he turned to Brantley and pushed a manila envelope over. "Your daughter has spent the last two nights with Mr. Wolfe."

Brantley had just hired the PI to start working on Monday, but two nights was two too many.

What about Brandon? Why isn't she taking the bait?

"She did meet with Brandon Taylor on Monday at the local diner. It appeared friendly. They then went to visit a farmer by the name of"—he pulled his notebook into his line of sight—"Dan Davis. I spoke to Mr. Davis after your daughter and Mr. Taylor left. It seemed they were looking to buy some land for a mobile park home."

What in the hell is Addison doing?

"But Mr. Davis told them no when Mr. Wolfe showed up," the detective continued. "After I left, I thought your daughter was going back to town, but I traced her cell to a field about a mile away from Mr. Davis's farm." He nodded to the envelope. "It seems she is very involved with Mr. Wolfe."

Brantley opened the envelope, and the contents spilled across the desk. Simon came around and looked at the photos that had been taken by the detective. His jaw clenched, similar to what Brantley figured his was doing.

"I apologize for the sensitive nature of the photos, but you can see that she is with Mr. Wolfe and not Mr. Taylor."

Brantley felt his blood pressure rising. With the return of Maddox Wolfe and Addison's lack of interest in Simon, Brantley had insisted her old boyfriend head up the golf course project. His plan was to lure her away from Maddox with Brandon and then lure her away from Brandon with Simon.

Nothing was going as planned. He was going to die with no one to run his company.

Maddox was supposed to hate his daughter for making his mother lose her home, and Addison was supposed to be with Brandon.

Brantley took the photos and pounded his fist on them.

It looked like he needed another plan.

It was time to get the Wolfe boy out of his daughter's life forever.

35

ADDISON

It was Sunday, and my weekly dinner with my father was hanging over my head. I hadn't discussed things with him yet for several reasons. If I went storming into his office, all pissed off, he wouldn't listen to a word I said. And he'd accuse me of being an emotional female.

And then part of me worried that me getting upset was his goal. If I went in and let him know I was mad, maybe I'd be giving him exactly what he wanted.

So, I needed a clear head before I went to speak to my father.

I almost considered letting it go because I knew he was doing this to get to me, but it wasn't in my nature to ignore it. I still felt like there was more I could have done twelve years ago, and I never wanted to feel like that again.

I arrived early, hoping to catch my father in his office. Of course, that was where he was. He was getting better since his stroke and was probably doing more than the doctor had given him permission to.

I knocked on the open door. If I wanted my father's full attention, I needed to be as respectful as possible. He was sitting at his desk with Simon standing next to him.

His head came up, and he smiled when he saw me. "Hello, Addison." He looked over at the clock on the wall and frowned. "You're early."

"Yes, I wanted to discuss something with you. Do you mind if I come in?"

"You may enter." He waved me toward him.

"Simon, do you mind if I talk to my father alone?"

He looked at my dad, who nodded, and Simon left the room.

Tucking my dress under my legs, I took a seat in front of him.

He folded his hands and looked at me. That was a little odd. Maybe he had been expecting this. "What can I help you with?"

"I wanted to talk to you about the golf course."

My father grinned. "Are you excited for it? It will bring a lot of business to our little town."

"Yes, it will. And I am looking forward to seeing it finished and up and running. But, Dad, I'm wondering why you expanded the plans."

"Pretty clever of me, huh? I wanted to find a way to keep the place going in the winter and on raining days. What better way than an indoor swimming pool, a gym, a couple of racquetball courts, and a restaurant? You get the idea."

"Yes, it's all wonderful."

My father had to know why I was here. He was never this talkative or this smiley. He was saying all these positive things to get me to sound like the bad guy when I brought up the trailer park.

It was no surprise that my father was a good businessman. He was very cunning.

"Dad, while all these things will be great for our community, what about the people who are going to lose their homes? You know many of them can't afford much." That was why they lived where they lived. "I'm worried they will have nowhere else to go."

"Addison, dear, as I understand it, they've been given sixty days to move. I think Brandon's company is being more than generous."

I clenched my jaw. He was blaming the company when this was his idea in the first place.

"Don't you think it's a little unfair? This golf course is supposed to help these people, and you're making it a challenge for them to keep living here."

My father met my eyes. "Addison, life is not fair. You should know that by now." He lifted his shoulders. "It's a necessary evil. It's for a good cause."

"You could help find them a new place to live. You own that land."

He held up a finger. "Correction: owned. I traded the land for shares in the new country club."

I felt like we were going around in circles. "You could buy new land. You could build a new park. You have the funds."

My father looked as if he were actually considering my words, but then he said, "No."

Just no. Nothing else.

I jumped up from my seat. "You're doing this because of Maddox, aren't you?"

"Whatever are you talking about? Maddox?"

I narrowed my eyes. He was trying to play dumb. I could see the corners of his mouth twitch.

I pointed a finger at him. "You know the golf course was my idea to begin with. You changed the plans, so Maddox's mom would lose her home. You hoped he would blame me."

My father looked up at me and leaned back in his seat. "I don't have a clue as to what you're talking about."

Liar.

"Besides, even if that was my plan, it didn't work, did it? Otherwise, you wouldn't be fucking the Wolfe boy in the back of his vehicle in some field in the country."

I sucked in my breath. I had never heard my father swear before, and he'd just used it to discuss what Maddox and I had done in private. What should have been a private moment.

"Are you following me?"

He spread his arms. "You know I don't leave the house much. I've been getting out more, but following you? Come on, Addison."

I hated it when he made me feel like a foolish child. "Excuse me. I meant, you're having me followed."

My father stood and pounded his fists on his desk. "I will do whatever I need to in order to make sure things are done right."

I crossed my arms over my chest. "Not right, Dad. The way you want them."

"*You're goddamn right*. And, if it means getting you away from Maddox Wolfe, then I'll do whatever I need to get him out of your life."

I shivered at my father's threat. I'd had no idea what lengths he would go to in order to keep us apart.

I dropped my arms and stood. I planted my hands on the

desk, getting in his face. "News flash: I'm not eighteen anymore. I'm thirty. You can't order me around."

His eyes flared. "I control your money."

I shrugged as if I didn't care, but it did worry me. "Go ahead and try. My trust fund is set up for my protection. You can try to get the board to stop disbursement, but not liking my boyfriend isn't going to sway them in your favor. I'm a respected member of this community, and I haven't done anything reckless or broken any laws."

"Daughter dear, you don't know how much power I wield."

Yes, unfortunately, I did.

I stepped back. "You do what you need to do. And I'll do what I need to do. You can't control me anymore." I clenched my fists. "I refuse to be controlled by you, and if I'm going to lose my money, so be it." I lowered my voice. "I'd rather be broke and free than rich and a prisoner."

I turned and walked toward the door.

"Addison, you're going to regret choosing that boy over your family."

I laughed and looked over my shoulder. "*Family* is a very generous word for what we are. Tell the cooks to put one less plate out at dinner. I'll be back when Maddox is welcome to sit next to me."

I quietly shut the office and ran into Simon on the way out of the house.

"You're making a big mistake, Addison."

I looked Simon up and down. "What's it to you?"

"Your father wants you to inherit his company."

"Yes, well, I don't want it." I pushed Simon out of the way. "Tell him he can give it all to you."

"He won't do that," Simon called after me.

I turned at the door. "You weren't in his office just now. I bet he'll do it." I pushed on the heavy wood and walked out of there.

The sun and the fresh air brought me a little peace. I didn't realize how trapped I'd felt until I walked out of my childhood home just now. Maybe telling my father to shove his money up his ass was more freeing than I'd thought.

As I drove back to my apartment, I did worry how I'd make ends meet if the board went along with my father's request. But I could save that worry for another day.

When I got home, rather than going to my apartment, I went next door. I needed to talk to Maddox. I knocked once and pushed open the door.

"Where the hell do you think you're going?" Maddox yelled.

"You're going the wrong way," Serena yelled back. "Follow me."

Smiling, I closed the door behind me and walked into the room.

Maddox looked up from the video game he and Serena were playing and hit pause. "What's going on, babe? I thought you were having dinner."

I plopped down on the couch next to Serena. "My dad and I got into it. I left."

"Uncle Maddox and I were going to order pizza. You can eat with us."

I smiled at her. "Thanks. I'd love that." I looked over at the kitchen counter. It was filled with guns and knives. "What's that?" I asked, slightly alarmed.

"Oh," Serena said, all excited. "Uncle Maddox showed me all his weapons. He's got some badass stuff." She set her controller down and hopped up from her seat. She grabbed a gun and pointed it at the wall.

I felt my eyes widen as I pushed myself back into the couch.

Maddox laughed. "Don't worry. It's not loaded."

"Uncle Maddox said he's going to take me shooting. I can't wait."

I looked at Maddox.

He shrugged. "It'll be good for her to learn to protect herself."

I guess.

Guns had always scared me.

Serena put the gun down and picked up another weapon that looked like a knife, and Maddox crooked a finger at me.

I scooted closer to him, and he put his arm around me.

"You okay?"

I sighed. "Actually, yeah. I think it's good. My father threatened to cut off my finances, but I feel like a weight has been lifted off my shoulders."

He brushed his lips over mine. "I'm glad."

I looked over at Serena, who now had a gun and a knife in her hands. "Are you sure she's okay to look at that stuff?"

Maddox looked over. "Yeah, she's fine." He turned back to me and put his mouth next to my ear. "Don't worry, baby. I'll show you my *special weapon* later tonight."

I laughed and snuggled into him. No matter what had happened with my father, I'd made the right decision.

36

MADDOX

After a particularly spectacular fucking session, Addison dragged me out of bed to attend Brook Days. I'd been back in town for a month now, and I'd spent every night in Addison's bed, or her in mine, for over the last two weeks.

"Why are you so happy?" I asked her as I held her hand and walked down the street.

Brook Days took place at the Brook Creek Middle and High School. Our town was too small to have two separate schools.

Every year that I could remember, the lawn was set up with the chili cook-off, horseshoes, and other games. There were a couple of concession stands selling lunch and snacks. The football field would be used for flag football later, the only event I wanted to participate in, and the baseball field would be used for baseball. The school was opened up for basketball and volleyball to be played inside.

"I like Brook Days," Addison said. "Creek Days is all about partying, but Brook Days is more about family and teamwork, which means less work for me. No bailing someone out of jail for cooking chili."

We made it to the school and went around back to where everything was set up. It looked like the same layout that I remembered from twelve years ago. People greeted Addison. Some of these people even said hi to me, too. They were slowly opening their minds to me being back.

"Hey, you two."

I turned to see Brandon approaching us. I supposed you could say I was slowly opening my mind to him. It was obvious that Brandon had no romantic interest in Addison, and she didn't have any in him, yet it bothered me how close they were. I thought I didn't like how he'd been in her life while I was gone. It pissed me off that he had been around when I wasn't.

"Hey, Brandon," Addison said with a smile.

"Hey," I said, putting my arm around her and yanking her back to my front. I laced my fingers together to keep her close.

"Are you guys participating in anything today?" Brandon asked.

Addison shook her head. "Just eating a bunch of chili."

"I'm going to play football. You?" I asked.

Please say yes.

It would be very satisfying to be able to tackle him a couple of times as I pretended to forget it was flag football.

Brandon shook his head. "I didn't play any sports in high school. Except golf," he said with a laugh.

Pussy.

Brandon frowned. "Addison, you didn't say your dad was judging the chili contest."

Both Addison and I spun around to see that her father was indeed sitting at the judges' table.

Addison's mouth dropped open. "I had no idea."

That's what happens when you no longer speak to your father.

She'd told me a little bit of her conversation with her father the last time she had been over there, but I didn't think she'd told me everything. All I knew was that it hadn't gone well, and she hadn't gone back since.

"Do you want to go and talk to him?" I asked.

I was pissed that this guy was the reason my mother was going to lose her home. Addison and I hadn't come up with any new solutions. But I felt bad that she was estranged from her only parent.

She stepped closer to me. "No, not right now."

That's right, baby. I'll protect you.

"That's okay, babe. You don't need to talk to him if you're not ready."

She didn't say anything, just continued to watch her father. "Sometimes, I wish he could be different."

I put my arm around her and kissed her forehead. "I understand that completely." I'd often wished my mom hadn't drunk when I was growing up. "Come on, let's go find something else to do."

As I turned her to go in the opposite direction, I saw the guy I'd seen hanging around her the night of the street dance. "Who is that again?"

Addison looked over and curled her lip. "That's Simon. He's my father's protégé, shadow, and personal ass-kisser."

"I take it, you don't like him."

"He's smarmy. He actually thinks that I might date him just because my father wants me to." She shivered and made a disgusted face. "I'd rather stick my hand in boiling water."

"Tell me how you really feel," I joked, but at the same time, I took inventory of the man. I didn't like that he hit on Addison, especially when she didn't want his advances. "He's never come to your apartment or anything, has he?"

She looked up at me. "No. He's never even come to my office before. Why? Should I be worried?"

I rubbed her arm and smiled at her. "No." I nodded my head to the left. "Let's go over there."

"Okay."

"Maddox, Maddox, Maddox," a voice shouted from behind me.

I turned around to see Ben.

I held up my hand for a high five. "Hey, buddy. How's it going?"

"Hey, Claire," Addison said beside me. "How are you?"

I nodded to her, and she smiled at both of us.

"I'm good. Thank you for the recommendations. Things are going well so far."

I looked at Addison, and she smiled. I didn't ask, but I sure hoped the two of them were talking about the custody case.

I felt a tugging on my arm and looked down.

"Are you going to have ice cream? Mom said she was going to buy me ice cream," Ben said.

"What? No fair." I got down on one knee and blocked my mouth but talked loud enough for her to hear. "I asked Addison if I could have some ice cream, but she told me I was too naughty."

"*Maddox*," Addison scolded me.

I peeked up at her to see her face turning bright red.

Ben tilted his head. "What did you do?"

"She says I'm a bed hog and that I take all the covers." I rolled my eyes for emphasis.

Ben shook his head and pointed to himself. "My mom says the same thing about me."

I threw my hands in the air. "And yet you still get ice cream. Your mom is nicer than Addison. You're one lucky guy."

Ben shook his head in disappointment as he looked at Addison.

I bit my lip to keep from laughing. "I bet your mom deserves a big thank-you for being so nice."

Ben turned around. "Thanks, Mom."

She smiled. "You're welcome." She held out her hand. "Shall we go?"

"Yeah." Ben held out his fist for me, and I bumped it. "Good luck, dude."

"Thanks. I might need it."

Ben took his mom's hand, and he skipped off with her.

I stood, and Addison backhanded me in the gut.

"Way to go. Now, the kid thinks I'm a big meanie."

I laughed. "You are a big meanie. 'Maddox, harder. Right there, Maddox. Don't stop.'" I mimicked her higher voice. "You're always bossing me around."

"You're such an asshole." She might have insulted me, but she was laughing, too.

"Who's ready to play some football?" a voice yelled in the crowd.

I clapped my hands together. "Come on, let's go over there."

Addison followed me over to the football field where people were crowding around to play. The person in charge had everyone line up and count off by ones and twos.

"All right," the leader said, "it's shirts versus skins. Ones are shirts. Twos are skins."

"That's me," I said and pulled my tee over my head. I handed it to Addison and turned toward the field to stretch.

Addison gasped and pushed my shirt into my chest. "You need to put this back on. Right now." Her eyes were huge.

I looked around for danger but didn't see anything. "Why?"

Her face was pinking up again. "Your back is covered in scratch marks. It's obvious I put them there."

I threw my head back and laughed.

"Maddox, this isn't funny."

"It kind of is." I laughed again. "Maybe, if you weren't so feisty in bed, I wouldn't be all scratched up."

She narrowed her eyes at me. "Yeah, well, maybe you shouldn't make me come so much."

I shook my head. "Never, babe. I'm always going to make you come."

A whistle blew.

"Gotta go." I slapped her on the ass. "Don't forget to cheer for me."

37

ADDISON

I watched Maddox run off to play football and put my hands to my cheeks. They felt like they were on fire.

I couldn't believe that Maddox was walking around with his shirt off. His back had new and old marks on it from my fingernails.

I held my hands out in front of me and spread my fingers. Maybe it was time to get a manicure. And I'd tell the technician to make sure she cut my nails as short as they could go.

I dropped my arms. Or maybe I should just be more aware of where my hands were when we were having sex.

Yeah, right. That wasn't going to happen.

That man got me so twisted up inside. The only things I knew when we did it was where my vagina and my mouth were. Someone could cut off my foot, and I wouldn't notice as long as Maddox Wolfe was inside me.

"He kind of makes you crazy, huh?"

I jumped and turned to see Kelly coming to stand beside me.

"Uh…yeah, he does. But in a good way."

I'd talked to Kelly before. She was the mother of my single employee, but it felt different. Now, I was talking to her as the sister of the guy I was sleeping with. Thankfully, we both were facing the game, which made it easier for me to talk to her.

"He'll do that to you. Growing up, he always knew what buttons to push with me."

"I imagine that's what little brothers are supposed to do," I said wistfully. I'd often wished I weren't an only child. It had been lonely, growing up in that big house with no one to play with.

"You really like him, don't you?"

"Yes." There was no point in denying it. I probably had lovesick puppy written all over my face.

"I can tell he really likes you, too." She turned to me, so I did the same. "I can tell you're a good person, Addison. You helped out Serena when she needed a job, and I know you're trying to make this town a better place."

"I sense a *but*."

She smiled but only for a moment. "But, if you hurt my brother again…" She shook her head. "I don't know what I'll do to you. Just please don't. He probably won't tell you, but twelve years ago, he was devastated. First, Foster and then you. It was a good thing the military gave him an outlet, I suppose."

I was shaking my head in confusion. I only understood about half of what she was saying. "Kelly, I'm not sure exactly what you're saying, but I'll do what I can to not hurt him."

She smiled. "Good. That's what I wanted to hear."

I was glad she was placated, but I didn't understand what

she meant about hurting her brother *again*. I didn't know there was a first time. I opened my mouth to ask her to expand on her earlier statement.

"Mom?" a voice called out from several feet away.

Kelly turned around and waved her arm in the air. "Over here."

Serena came through the crowd, holding on to Maddox's mom's arm. Foster was walking up behind them.

"Hello, Mrs. Wolfe," I said. "Hi, Serena."

"You can call me Betty, dear."

"Hello, Betty," I said.

It was a change from the woman I remembered from when Maddox and I'd dated in high school. I still remembered when she'd come home one night while I was in Maddox's room. I'd been hiding in his room, and she'd called me a slut while she was arguing with Maddox. She'd been drunk at the time, and she probably had no recollection of it, but at seventeen, I would never forget it.

"Are you having a nice time?" I asked her.

I was glad for Betty and her children that she had gotten sober. I didn't see her around town much, but I knew she was sick. The day I'd gone to her house and asked for a dollar was the first time I saw her in months, and I had been in a rush, so I hadn't stuck around to chat.

"Yes. It feels good to be outside." She lifted an arm to shield her eyes from the sun. "Is that my Maddox playing out there?"

"Yep. He's showing off his old football tricks." I looked over at the field. "Or at least, he's trying to." I looked back at Betty. "I don't know what he's told you, but I'm doing everything I can, so you don't lose your home or your place to live."

Betty grabbed my hand and squeezed. Her skin was cold and rough. "He's told me that you've been working your ass off."

I laughed at hearing her say *ass*.

"Don't worry about me. I can always move in with one of my children if I have to."

Both Kelly's and Foster's eyes got big. I took it that this was news to them, and neither of them looked too thrilled with the idea.

"Hey, Mom, I'm going to go hang out with my friends," Serena said.

"Sure."

Serena kissed Betty on the cheek. "I'll see you later, Grandma."

"Okay, dear. Go have fun."

Serena ran off and joined a couple of girls her age.

The whistle blew behind us, and we all turned to see what was going on with the game. Maddox came running over to us. The first thing he did was kiss his mom on the cheek, and it made me smile. He was a good son.

He nodded to his brother's water. "Do you mind if I have some of that?"

Foster handed it over. "It's all yours. I can get another."

Maddox opened the bottle and drank all of it. I hoped no one noticed me staring at the way some of the water escaped and ran down his throat and onto his chest.

Kelly nudged me with her hip. "Your mouth's open," she whispered with a laugh.

I snapped my jaw shut, and once again, I turned red. I couldn't remember the last time I had blushed, but today, I was on a roll.

There was a garbage can about five feet from us, and

Maddox threw the empty bottle toward it. Of course, he made it.

"Hey, you should come and play with us," Maddox said to Foster, nodding toward the field.

Foster had played football in middle school and the first two years of high school. He hadn't been as good as Maddox, and he had stopped playing when he got involved with partying and drinking.

"Sure. Sounds like fun. I'll be on the shirts team. Then, I can kick your ass."

Maddox grinned. "You wish. You just don't want to show off your pudgy body."

Foster lifted the front of his shirt and showed off an impressive four-pack. "Pudgy body, my ass."

"Boys, boys." Betty rolled her eyes. "They never stop fighting."

Despite the past, Maddox was lucky to have Foster. They obviously loved each other despite their bickering.

Maddox put his arm around me and kissed the side of my head. "You doing okay, babe?" he asked me in a low voice.

I wrapped my arm around his waist and squeezed. "Yeah, I'm doing good."

"Good." He dropped his arm and stepped back toward the field. "Come on, Foster. Let's see who needs another teammate."

Maddox turned, and Foster followed.

"Oh my word, Maddox. You need to be more careful out there," Betty said.

Maddox looked over his shoulder at his mother with a puzzled expression on his face.

Betty pointed. "Your back, son. It's all scratched up."

Maddox barked out a laugh while I turned red. Again.

38

MADDOX

Sunday afternoon, there was a knock at my door. I'd just gotten back from brunch at my sister's, and Addison was spending the day with friends. I opened my door to see the last person I'd expected.

"Hello. I'm Simon Deavor, and I work—"

"I know who you are and who you work for." I crossed my arms over my chest. "What do you want?"

Simon pursed his lips at my rudeness. I hoped he'd take the hint and leave.

"Mr. Graham would like to speak to you."

I had to admit, this surprised me, but I didn't let it show. "Tell him no, thank you." I dropped my arms and grabbed the door to slam it in Simon's face.

He slapped his hand against it. "I think you'll want to hear this. It concerns your mother."

Fuck.

There was nothing good that could come from this conversation.

Once we arrived at the Graham home, Simon directed me toward the home office, and I tried my best not to look around in awe at the house Addison had grown up in even though I'd seen it years ago. I'd forgotten just how big it was. We'd had such different childhoods.

Once I reached the wooden double doors, Simon opened them and instructed me in.

Brantley Graham sat on the other end of his huge desk and smiled like we were old friends or something. "Ah, Mr. Wolfe, come in, please."

When I reached the desk, Brantley swept his arm out. "Please sit."

"I'll stand, thank you."

"Very well," he said, losing some of his smile.

I pointed to Simon behind me. "Your errand boy over there said you wanted to talk to me about my mother."

"Yes. As I understand it, she hasn't found a new home yet."

I gritted my teeth. "No."

"I'm sorry your mom had to become involved in the mess, but I saw a good opportunity for our town, and I couldn't pass on it."

This guy was feeding me some serious bullshit. Addison had told me how long she'd been trying to get her father to sell the land to the golf course company. Obviously, Brantley was up to something.

When I didn't say anything, he continued, "I have decided to help your mother."

"And what will it cost me?" I asked.

Brantley chuckled and then acted shocked.

"I might not be rich, Brantley, but I'm not stupid. You purposely asked me here when Addison was in Des Moines, and you knew I'd be alone. You want something in return."

He raised his brow. "Okay, if that's how you want to play it." He looked around me. "Simon, bring me the envelope."

I turned to watch Simon take a manila envelope off the shelf and bring it to me.

"I suggest you open that carefully, Mr. Wolfe."

I slowly opened the envelope and slid out the contents. It was pictures of Addison and me. In very compromising positions. I squeezed my fist around them, furious. Someone had spied on our personal moments. Someone had taken pictures of Addison naked. And Addison had been betrayed by someone she should have been able to trust.

Her father was far worse than I'd ever thought.

"What the fuck do you want, Brantley?"

He stood. "I want you to stay away from my daughter." He grabbed a piece of paper and threw it to my side of the desk. It was a real estate sheet of a house here in town. "You break things off with Addison, and I will buy this for your mother to live in. She can live there, rent-free."

Until Brantley Graham was unhappy with something, and then he'd kick my mom out.

"And what about the other trailer park residents?"

Brantley shrugged. "I don't wish them ill. They are simply a means to an end. I already gave away the land. There is nothing I can do."

This guy was a heartless prick, but he had me thinking. My mom was sick. She needed a home.

I saw Brantley smile out of the corner of my eye, and I wanted to punch him.

"Mr. Wolfe?"

I looked up.

He slid a smaller piece of paper over to me. "Here is a little more incentive to help you accept my conditions."

I picked it up and flipped it over. It was a check for more money than I'd made in a whole year as a Navy SEAL. I looked up at Brantley as if to confirm it was real.

He raised his eyebrows. "I'll double that, but then that's as high as I'll go."

The guy made me sick.

I put the photos, the home info sheet, and the check all in the manila envelope.

I could see the look of satisfaction on Brantley Graham's face, and it took all my willpower to not slam his face on the desk.

"I take it, we have an understanding?" he asked me.

I took the envelope and walked over to the paper shredder I'd noticed in the corner. I pushed the envelope in the slot and watched as the automatic motor pulled it down and shredded the photos, the home sheet, and the check.

When the motor quieted, I looked up at Brantley. "Yes, we have an understanding. Your daughter means more to me than money, and there is nothing you can do to keep me away from her."

He narrowed his eyes at me. "Even if it costs your mother a place to live?"

I shook my head and laughed. As if my mother didn't have other options. "You let me worry about my mom." I headed for the door. "If I were you, I'd worry about what your daughter is going to think when she hears this." I reached the door and looked over at Simon. "See you later, errand boy."

I shoved the door open and escaped from the house. I took one last look at it before I got in my SUV.

Poor Addison. All the money in the world wouldn't make up for having a father like Brantley.

As I drove away, I picked up my phone and dialed.

"Hello?"

"Hey, baby. How's it going?"

"Good. How are you? Enjoying your day off?"

I had to talk to her about her father, but I didn't want to do it over the phone. "It's fine."

"Are you okay?" Her voice changed, now sounding concerned.

I smiled that she knew me well enough to know something was wrong. "Yeah, I just needed to hear your voice."

"You're so sweet."

"Don't tell anyone, okay?"

She laughed.

"You'll be home tomorrow morning?"

"Yep. Bright and early."

"Okay. Come say hi when you get back, all right?"

"Promise."

I hung up the phone, feeling a little bit better but dreading the conversation I was going to have with her in the morning.

39

ADDISON

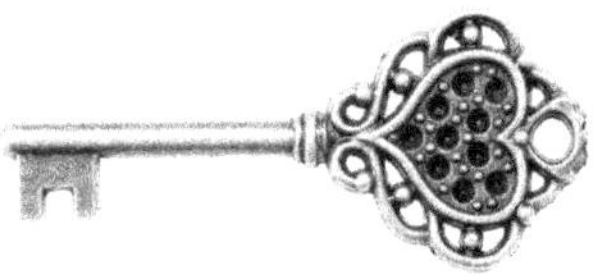

I wish I were able to sneak into Maddox's room like he was able to sneak into mine. I supposed I needed some military training in order to know how to do that. Instead, I pulled out the old spare key I had from when the Carson brothers had lived there. I had taken care of their dog a couple of times while they were on vacation. I just hoped the key still worked.

It worked but not without some jiggling.

Damn these old doors and old locks.

I pushed the door open and was greeted by darkness. It was only about ten at night, but Maddox must have already gone to bed. I was glad that I had used the key instead of knocking. I padded quietly into the room and shut the door.

The moment the latch clicked, a hand went around my mouth, and a hard body slammed me into the wall. I tried to yell out in fright.

"Addison?"

It was Maddox.

"Yes," I said, but it came out muffled.

He dropped his hand and spun me around. My eyes had adjusted to the light. I could see a gun in one hand, thankfully pointed away from me.

I heard him flick the safety on.

"What are you doing here?"

"I came back early."

He chuckled. "Yeah, I can see that. But why?"

I put my hands on his chest. *Ooh, it's bare.* I dragged my fingers down, down, down. "I wanted to see you," I told him.

He brushed his lips against mine. "What are you doing?"

"Checking to see if you're naked."

He pushed his pelvis into me. "Spoiler alert: I am."

I gasped as I took his length in my hand. "You're hard."

He nuzzled my neck. "Adrenaline. Plus, a hot woman just snuck into my apartment." He sucked on my skin.

"Wow. You're so lucky. What are you going to do to her?"

He chuckled again and put his mouth next to my ear. "Fuck her, of course."

Maddox set his gun down on the bookshelf next to him and attacked my shorts and underwear. He yanked them down my legs, and I helped by trying to kick them off. He picked me up, I wrapped my legs around his waist, and he slammed into me.

My head fell back and hit the wall. "*Ah.*" I hadn't quite expected that.

Maddox used one hand to hold me up and the other to pull down the straps of my tank top and bra. When my breasts were uncovered, he sucked one nipple into his mouth.

My pussy clamped down on him in immediate reaction, and I felt him smile against my skin.

"Have I ever told you how much I love how you respond to me?" he asked as he gripped my hips and pounded into me.

I shook my head and tightened my thighs on his hips. I couldn't move my arms any higher because my tank top and bra had them pinned to my sides. "I don't know."

He laughed. "Rhetorical question, baby." He kissed me. "But I do."

"Have I ever told you how much I love how you fuck me?" I returned.

"Only every time I'm inside you."

I dug my nails into his sides as he shifted and entered me at a new angle. I opened my mouth as little gasps escaped.

"You close, Addy?"

"Uh…uh…" I nodded.

Maddox sucked my other nipple into his mouth and then let it go with a pop. "Yeah, you are. I can feel it." He kissed between my breasts and up my chest. He kissed the front of my throat and around to the other side of my neck. "You want me to come inside you, Addy?"

I squeezed his cock with my pussy.

"Yeah, you like it when I come in you, don't you?"

I could hear the grin in his voice.

I did. I really did. I'd always practiced safe sex, except with Maddox. If he ever tried to use a condom, I'd probably rip it off him.

"Yeah, I love coming in your bare pussy, too. I love knowing that my cum is inside you. I hope other males can smell it on you, so they know you're mine."

I screamed out and clutched Maddox to me as I came.

He pushed me hard against the wall, spread my legs out,

and shoved inside me one last time as he exploded, filling me with his seed.

After we both caught our breaths, Maddox gently set my legs on the ground. I was grateful for the care, as they were shaking from having sex and the position they'd been in.

Maddox took my tank top and bra off and threw them behind him. "Better." He ran his hand down my throat and to my crotch where he pushed two fingers into me. He was gentle but thorough.

I gasped and clutched his biceps.

He pulled his hand away and then stuck his fingers in my mouth. This wasn't the first time he'd done that, and I loved watching the heat flare in his eyes when I seized hold of his hand and sucked his fingers clean.

He growled and kissed me, and I shared the taste of us with him.

He drew his mouth away, grabbed his gun, and picked me up under my knees.

I laughed. "What are you doing?"

"Taking you to bed."

I sighed in contentment and rested my head on his shoulder. "Okay."

He laid me down in his big bed, put his gun in the nightstand, and got in next to me.

"Why the gun when I got back tonight?" I understood he'd thought someone might be breaking in, but it seemed kind of extreme.

He put his arms behind his head. "It's going to sound weird, but after I got back from working out this afternoon, I swear, someone had been in my apartment."

I shivered. The whole thought of someone being in my

personal space without my knowledge creeped me out. "Was anything missing or out of place?"

"Not at first glance, no. And I haven't gone through everything, but I can't shake the feeling. It might sound odd, but in the military, I learned to rely on my instincts."

I put my hand on his chest. "I don't think it's odd. Who do you think it was?"

He shrugged. "I have no idea."

Something about the way he'd said that had me questioning his honesty. "You're not telling me something."

A heavy sigh. "That's because I don't know how to tell you."

I was on alert. This didn't sound like it was going to be good.

"You know how I called you this afternoon?"

"Yes."

He hadn't sounded like himself.

"I had just left your father's."

This had me sitting up. "*What*?"

Maddox then proceeded to tell me everything that had happened.

"What an asshole! He actually offered you money to stay away from me?"

He grasped my hand and squeezed.

"And someone watched us have sex and took pictures." I shuddered again. "It's a good thing we haven't been screwing all over town, or he'd have enough pictures to make a scrapbook."

"I'm sorry, Addy. I hate that someone saw us like that."

I squeezed his fingers back. "It's *not* your fault. My father...well, he's something else." Something occurred to me. "You don't think my father was the one in your apartment, do you?"

"I don't know. Obviously, your father is lacking a few morals, but I can't see him breaking in here. This is going to sound crazy, but I feel like he would think it's beneath him."

I laughed. "No, I totally understand what you mean. It doesn't seem like my father. Bribery and blackmail are his style. Breaking and entering are below his usual standards." I lay back down, half on Maddox, half on the bed. "What are you going to do?"

"I didn't think to call the Carsons. Maybe one of them stopped in." His shoulder shrugged under my head. "I can hope anyway."

I hoped, too, but I didn't have a good feeling about it. I could hear in Maddox's voice that he didn't either.

40

MADDOX

Addison left my bed around seven in the morning after being glued to my side all night. I loved sleeping with that woman, but I was going to have to invest in another fan. She sure made me hot. So much that it always woke me once or twice in the night.

But I just used it as a chance to make love to her. If she was going to wake me up even if it wasn't purposely, she was going to give me her body. She never complained though, and I suspected she liked it.

I just stepped out of the shower when there was a knock at my door.

"One minute," I yelled out of my open bathroom as I quickly threw on a pair of shorts and a T-shirt.

I took a quick glance at my watch to see it was only eight in the morning right before I opened the door.

Who'd be here this early?

There, standing on the landing, was Sheriff Whitlock with a pair of handcuffs in his hands.

"Maddox Wolfe?"

"You already know who I am."

Prick.

"Please step outside and put your hands behind your back."

"What the hell for?"

"You're under arrest."

Not again.

"I repeat, what the hell for?"

"The attempted murder of Brandon Taylor."

Addison's ex?

I had a sinking feeling that I was in a shitload of trouble.

"Where were you last night?"

It was twelve years ago all over again.

"Home."

I sat in the interrogation room, handcuffed to the table like I was some sort of threat.

"Go through your day with me."

"I woke up and went to my sister's for brunch. I got home a little after noon, and Brantley's lapdog asked me to come to Mr. Graham's house."

Whitlock snickered, and I knew he didn't believe me about going to Graham's house. To be fair, I wouldn't have believed me either.

"Then, I went and worked out, came home and showered, and spent the rest of the evening at home, alone."

"What about during the middle of the night?" The sheriff picked up a piece of paper and squinted. "Between the hours of eleven p.m. and six a.m.?"

I gritted my teeth. I didn't want to say it, but it was the truth. "I was with Addison," I said through clenched teeth.

Whitlock hooted with laughter. "I've seen the two of you around town together, but if you think she's going to alibi you…" He laughed again. "Well, you know what happens when it comes to her vouching for you." His laughter died, and he smiled at me. "Don't you?"

I calmed myself. I knew Whitlock wanted to rile me up. I knew he wanted me to get mad. He wanted me to mess up somehow. Good thing for me, I'd been through SERE—Survival, Evasion, Resistance, and Escape—training. I could take whatever this asshole threw at me. As long as I didn't let my soft spot—Addison—be affected too much.

I shrugged. "I guess we'll see." I looked toward the two-way mirror. "Have you called her yet?" I asked casually. "She's kind of my lawyer, too."

"Well, asshole, if you were with Addison last night, then why the hell did we find a handgun registered to you at the scene?"

Fuck. I had been right about someone being in my apartment. And it was worse than I could even imagine.

"I have a question for you," I said. "Why would I shoot someone and leave my gun there, only to be caught? I'm obviously being set up."

The sheriff shrugged. "Maybe you're an idiot. Maybe he scared you, and you dropped it. I don't know why you left your fucking weapon there. I just know you did. We have you red-handed. If you confess now, I'll get them to go easy on you."

Yeah, right.

"And what's my motive?" I challenged him, ignoring his question.

Whitlock shrugged. "He's fucking your girl."

Don't get mad, Wolfe. This jack-off is not worth it.

"He used to fuck her. He's not fucking her now because she spends every night in my bed."

"Except last night," he said with a smirk. "Rumor has it, she was out of town."

"She came back early."

"You wish. But, even if she did, like I said, you're probably on your own again. Just like you were twelve years ago." He sat back in his seat and crossed his arms. "I know you think she'll come forward because she held your hand at Brook Days. But this is her career, man. She's not going to risk it for some loser like you."

I knew the sheriff was just trying to goad me. I knew he was spewing shit from his mouth.

But there was a part of me that did worry. Would she come through for me?

Twelve years ago, she had been barely eighteen. She was thirty years old now. I'd seen her go to bat for her clients. She would do the same for me.

I hope.

And that little sliver of doubt had me wanting to jump over the table and strangle Sheriff Whitlock.

Part of me was glad I was in chains. It helped stop me from doing something stupid, and it would stop Whitlock from being right about the kind of person I was.

Yes, I had been jealous of Brandon a couple of times, but I'd never thought about murdering him. And, if I had, I sure as shit wouldn't have been so stupid as to leave my weapon behind.

One thing was for sure. I needed to get the hell out of

there. I would never find out who wanted me behind bars otherwise. And I would never be able to clear my name.

Because, even if Addison alibied me, my gun was a very strong reason to convict me.

I looked Whitlock in the eyes. "I think I'd like my lawyer now."

"Suit yourself. Don't come crying to me when you're looking at twenty-five to life."

I didn't say a word.

Whitlock pushed back his chair and stood. "You're making a big mistake."

I continued to stare.

The sheriff went to the door and opened it. "Get this asshole his lawyer. Get Addison Graham down here now."

41

ADDISON

When I heard the news about Brandon, I rushed over to the motel. Being that Brook Creek is a small town, news traveled like wildfire. I made it there just as they were loading Brandon into the ambulance.

I tried to talk to him, but he was unconscious. He was bleeding from his head, and the paramedics said he'd been shot. I started crying because the nearest hospital was about twenty to thirty minutes away. And, even then, the town was only about sixteen thousand people. It wasn't a big hospital, and he'd probably have to be stabilized and moved to Des Moines.

I went back to my office, feeling sad and hopeless. My friend could die, and there wasn't anything I could do about it, except call his parents. That was the worst phone call I'd ever had to make, and I never wanted to have to do that again.

In a daze, I was sitting and staring at my computer. I should be working on stuff, but I felt like my brain was mush.

I hadn't even noticed that Serena hadn't come into work until she ran through the door, dread written all over her face.

I sprang from my chair. "What's wrong?"

I immediately thought that Brandon had died, and I was in such a panic that I didn't even consider the fact that, if that had happened, I would probably know before Serena.

"Sheriff..." She took a couple of deep breaths. "Sheriff Whitlock arrested Uncle Maddox."

"Why?" I had just seen the man less than two hours ago.

"For attempted murder. The sheriff says he's responsible for Brandon."

"That's crazy!"

"I know, but apparently, he has evidence."

I snatched my purse from the table in my office. I needed to get down to the sheriff's station.

At the same time, my phone rang.

"Addison Graham." *Please be quick.*

"This is Deputy McAllister. Your client is requesting your presence."

"Who is the client?"

"Maddox Wolfe."

Good man. He knew to call me.

"I'll be there in five. Wait."

"Yes?"

"Did the sheriff have you call me right away?"

Deputy McAllister hesitated. "No, ma'am."

Ma'am?

He was only three years younger than me.

"Thank you. And, Deputy?"

"Yes, ma'am?"

"Call me ma'am again, and I'll sue you for so many things that you'll be tied up in court for years."

I pushed the button to hang up the phone and released it. Once I heard the dial tone, I called in a favor from a classmate from college, and then I rushed to the sheriff's station.

Of course, good ole Sheriff Whitlock was there to greet me.

"His bail hearing is set at nine fifteen."

I looked at the clock. "That's in fifteen minutes." I wouldn't have any time to prepare.

The sheriff shrugged like it was out of his control when he was probably doing this on purpose. He scratched his head. "You can wait, but I think the next one is at six."

"P.M.?"

He smirked. "A.M."

Motherfucker.

"Fine. Nine fifteen it is."

I had to use all of my professionalism when I saw Maddox walk into the courtroom. He held his shoulders high, but I could see the defeat in his eyes.

Oh, baby, I promise I'm not going to let them take you away from me again.

When he saw me, the relief and happiness that crossed his face made my heart race. Despite the circumstances, that look told me so many things, including how he felt about me.

He came to stand next to me.

"How are you?" I asked. "I'm sorry I couldn't see you until now." I looked over at the sheriff and narrowed my eyes. "I wasn't given much warning about your bail hearing."

"It's okay, Addy. I'm just glad to see you."

The judge banged on the gavel, and we proceeded with the hearing.

Using my mother's jewelry I'd inherited as collateral for his bond, and an hour later, Maddox was free.

I waited for him to be released from the jail.

He walked out, rubbing his wrists where the handcuffs had been. He looked up at me, and I gave him a sad smile.

My handsome Maddox. He deserved so much better than this.

"I'll pay you back," he said when he reached me.

"Just show up for court, and we'll be fine," I joked. "I know you've been put through the wringer, but I was hoping we could go back to my office and get started on your case."

"Yeah. I don't think I could relax now if I tried."

We took off and walked toward my car. It was weird how awkward things were with us at the moment. I'd pretty much used him as a pillow last night, and now, we were walking a respectable distance apart like we barely knew each other.

"Brandon was attacked last night," he said when we almost reached my vehicle.

"I know. I told the sheriff you were with me, but your gun is pretty damning evidence. I'm guessing you were right about someone being in your apartment." I stopped walking and turned around because Maddox was no longer next to me. "What's wrong? Why'd you stop?"

He swallowed. "You told Whitlock you were with me?"

"Of course." I rolled my eyes. "He didn't believe me, obviously. But don't worry; we're going to get you out of this."

Maddox stepped forward and rubbed his thumb over my cheek. I didn't understand why he was being so tender, but it made my heart ache because he was being punished for something he hadn't done.

I put my hand on his. "We're going to fight this. I called in one badass criminal defense attorney to handle your case."

He frowned. "How come you know all these guys?"

"What do you mean?"

"First, Brandon, and now, this defense attorney..."

I laughed. "Who said the attorney was a guy?"

42

MADDOX

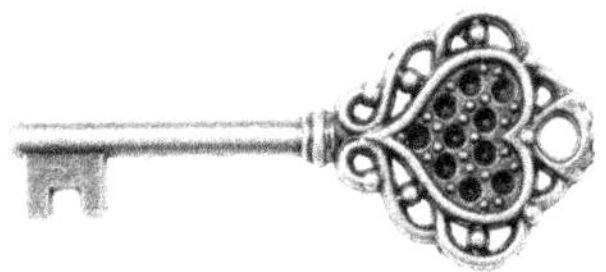

One of the best attorneys in the state of Iowa, according to Addison, was a small Asian woman. Olivia Mayer had to be about five-two and the size of a toothpick. She looked like she was about twelve years old, and I could see that people probably underestimated her by her appearance.

Addison sat behind her desk, taking notes, while I went over everything that had happened with my new lawyer.

"Did they do a gunshot residue test on you?" she asked me.

"No. Fucking dick."

She nodded to her assistant, a young guy who looked to be in his early twenties. "Make sure the state police does one."

Addison sat forward in her chair. "State police?"

Olivia smiled like the Cheshire cat. "You're not the only one with connections." She turned to me. "On the drive here, I took a look at your old case. Your court-appointed attorney was subpar, but he kept excellent records. Anyone can tell by the surveillance video that it wasn't you in the gas station." She tilted her head to the side. "What is it with you and people borrowing your stuff to commit crimes?"

I laughed because it was better than getting pissed. "I don't know."

I did know though. My brother, under the influence of alcohol, had borrowed my stuff like an idiot. He hadn't set out to make it look like it was me, but his drunk brain was only thinking about himself. This time, someone had set out to make me look guilty.

"Well, it's obvious the sheriff is biased, so I called in someone who isn't affiliated with this town or its history. We need fresh, objective eyes. Even with the video from the gas station and Addison alibiing you, the sheriff never looked at anyone else for the crime."

My eyes quickly went to Addison, who was nodding.

"When I went in and told the sheriff that I was with Maddox that night, I could tell that he wasn't listening to me. I can't believe he keeps getting elected."

"That's what happens when no one runs against you," Olivia said. "At least, that's the info I got online."

"No, it's true. No one wants to do that kind of job anymore. They all want the big-city life." Addison looked over at me. "Maddox, are you okay? You look a little pale."

While the two women had been discussing the sheriff, I was stuck on Addison talking about how she'd alibied me.

I looked at Olivia. "Can you excuse us a moment?"

She hesitated. "Anything you say to Addison, you really should say to me. While Addison will be working on this case with me, I'm going to be first chair at your trial if this case comes to that."

I shook my head. "I don't need to talk to her as my lawyer. I need to talk to her as my woman."

A knowing look passed over her eyes. "Ah. Okay. Derek?" she said to her assistant. "Let's go find something for lunch." The two of them stood. "We'll be back in thirty minutes."

I nodded, and the two walked out the door.

I got up from my chair as soon as I heard the click of the latch being closed, and Addison did the same. We met on the side of her desk.

"What's wrong?"

I clutched her hands in mine. "I have a question. No matter what, I won't be mad at how you answer. I just need to know the truth."

She looked worried, and I supposed I was scaring her with my intensity. But this was important.

"Okay."

"Twelve years ago…" I closed my eyes and swallowed. I opened them and asked, "Twelve years ago, you told the sheriff you were with me the night of the robbery?"

Her eyes filled with confusion and sympathy. "Of course I did, Maddox."

"But you never came to my trial."

"I didn't even know you had one. I went to visit my mom's parents, and when I got back, it was over, and you were gone." She shrugged. "I'd always thought your lawyer would make me come in and testify. After I started law school, I wondered why I was never subpoenaed."

I let go of her hands and shoved my fingers through my hair. Things were starting to fall into place. "I asked my lawyer not to subpoena you. I asked him to give you the option to testify. I wanted you to make the choice on your own. I didn't want to make you do anything." I thought my eighteen-year-old self had wanted to know that I was worth it for her to go against her father.

"I don't understand. Your lawyer never even asked me. I would have remembered."

"No, he did. He personally delivered a notice of appearance to your dad."

Fire lit her eyes. "Are you fucking serious?"

"That's what I was told."

She kicked the side of her desk. "*That motherfucking asshole*!"

Whoa.

I actually took a step back.

Her eyes narrowed. "He told me my grandma was sick. I'd thought it was odd because, when I got there, she seemed fine." She collapsed to the floor and put her head in her hands. "I can't believe him." She started to cry.

I sat down next to her and pulled her into my arms. "Shh. Baby, it's okay."

"No, it's not." She pulled out of my embrace and looked at me. "All these years…you thought I'd left you hanging out to dry, didn't you?"

I didn't want to say yes. She looked so heartbroken.

"You did. I can see it in your eyes." She swiped the back of her hand over her cheek. "I wondered why you were so mad at me when you came back to town." She laughed, but it was completely without humor. "I was so angry with you. I never stopped to really think about what had happened all those years ago."

I furrowed my brows. "You were angry with me?"

She laughed at me. "Yes. I loved you, Maddox. With all my heart. I was devastated when I never saw you again. I did everything I could to find you. But you had a closed trial, and the proceedings were sealed along with your record. I couldn't find any record of you in any prison. Then, I found out you'd been freed and in the military the whole time. I was very hurt." She looked down at her hands. "I never quite got over you. You were my first love. You were even the reason I became a lawyer. I kind of feel like my adult life has been a lie."

I picked up her hand and laced our fingers together. "I know you said a lot of stuff right now, but I'm kind of stuck on the *you loved me* part."

She laid her head on my shoulder. "It's not a surprise. I told you that I loved you back then."

I brushed my thumb over her hand, staring at the place we were connected. "I think it's the past-tense part. I don't want you to have loved me. I want you to love me. Now."

Addison lifted her head and laughed. "You big dummy. Of course I love you."

43

ADDISON

"Well"—Maddox raised his eyebrows—"it's not every day I get called a dummy and someone professes their love to me, all in the same sentence."

I snort-giggled. "I'm sorry. I'm a little emotional right now. I've just found out my father is the world's biggest asshole."

"Ah, baby," he said as he put his arm around me. "You deserve a better father. And you deserve better than me. I should have reached out to you over the years."

I sniffled. "Yes, you should have," I joked.

"I was just so..." He sighed. "I felt betrayed. I felt like... like I wasn't enough."

I wrapped my arms around him. "You are more than enough. I am so sorry."

I pictured Maddox as I had known him back then, probably scared and alone and thinking that I'd ditched him.

And wouldn't you know it? I started crying again.

He lifted my chin. "Addy, why all the tears?"

"I feel so bad for you."

Maddox laughed, and I narrowed my eyes at him.

"Don't feel bad for me. Everything turned out okay. I loved being in the military. I never cared for school, and I would have hated college. I found my calling."

"But all those years…we can never get them back."

He brushed the tears from my cheeks. "No, baby, we can't. But we're here now. And you love me, and I love you. No matter what happens, I will die happy, knowing that."

I launched myself in his arms and kissed him.

He loves me.

Maddox rolled me onto my back, and I reached for his belt. As I unbuckled, unzipped, and pushed down his pants, he pushed up my skirt and ripped my thong from between my legs. In one smooth thrust, he was inside me.

I crossed my ankles behind his back, and I had to laugh because I still had my high heels on. I felt a little bit like a porn star. But then Maddox hit the sweet spot inside me, and I forgot everything else.

He put his hand over my mouth and chuckled in my ear. "Shh…baby, my niece is right on the other side of the door."

I shook his hand off. "I can't help it. You feel too good inside me."

"Fucking music to my ears, but I don't want to scar her for life."

I laughed, and it turned into a moan.

Up Maddox's hand went again. "God, I want to spend all day naked with you, inside you, but your friend is going to be back soon. I apologize for the quick fuck, baby. I'll make it up to you later."

I nodded.

"I'll keep my hand here. You scream all you want."

And scream I did.

I watched Maddox through the one-way glass as a detective from the state police interviewed him. Olivia sat beside him as questions were asked. Detective Porter seemed like a no-nonsense kind of man. He was a big black man, who was pleasant when he smiled but scary when he frowned. I sure wouldn't dare commit a crime in front of him, but I admired the way he treated Maddox with respect even though he was a suspect.

The state police had already brought someone in to do a handgun residue test, although it was probably too late for that now. And Maddox gave them permission to search his place and to take his dirty laundry to the lab for testing.

Sheriff Whitlock stood beside me, fuming.

I crossed my arms over my chest. "Why is it that the state has done more investigative work in the two hours they've been here than you've done in your whole life?"

"I'd watch my mouth if I were you, young lady."

I snorted. "What are you going to do? Arrest me for telling the truth?" I turned to face him. "You knew Maddox was innocent all those years ago. Agnes Weller would be able to look at that surveillance tape and know it wasn't Maddox."

Agnes was the town's oldest resident. Someone had thrown her a birthday bash every year since she turned ninety, and she was now one hundred one. She was also blind as a bat.

The sheriff pulled at the waistband of his pants and raised his chin. "I know no such thing."

"You can lie to me all you want, but we both know the truth. You know I came here and told you Maddox was with me, but you never turned that evidence over to the DA, did you? No. You went to my father instead."

I hadn't been sure it was true until I saw the look on the sheriff's face right at that moment. So, my father must have already been planning to keep me away from Maddox's trial. And, when his lawyer had shown up, my father had shipped me off to my grandparents'.

I was furious at what both these men had done, but I thought the worst thing was, I'd never had a chance to say good-bye to Maddox.

"You're both despicable human beings. You almost sent an innocent man off to spend twenty years in prison."

Sheriff Whitlock narrowed his eyes at me. "He's not innocent."

"He's certainly not guilty." I didn't understand it. I knew why my father wanted Maddox out of my life, but I didn't understand why the sheriff hated him so much. It almost felt personal. "Why do you dislike Maddox? What did he do to make you hate him?"

The sheriff turned back to the interview in the other room. "I don't hate him."

"Sheriff?"

He looked at me.

"You're in law enforcement. You know a classic sign of lying is lack of eye contact. Why do you hate Maddox?"

At first, I didn't think he was going to answer.

But then he shocked the hell out of me when he said, "Did you know I used to be in love with Betty Wolfe?"

I held my breath, not knowing if I should actually answer. I was a little scared he'd stop talking if I said anything.

"Kelly was little, and her dad had run off. I helped Betty

out a time or two with things around her house, and we became friends. Before long, I was taking her out to the movies and dinner. I was completely infatuated with her. And I loved Kelly like she was my own."

He stopped. I was afraid he wouldn't continue for a moment, but I thought he had to get control of his emotions. I'd never seen the sheriff like this before.

"I went out and bought a ring. A beautiful diamond that I'd saved up for. Three months' pay went into that thing. Then, the night I was going to propose, she told me she was pregnant."

I sucked in a breath as my eyes went wide. I looked to the sheriff and to Maddox and back to the sheriff. I never knew who Maddox's father was.

Is the sheriff saying…

"No. You can get that look off your face," the sheriff said to me. "You see, Betty would never have…relations with me. She told me that she'd gotten pregnant with Kelly out of wedlock. She said that she wanted to wait. Turned out, she just didn't want to sleep with me."

"So, you blame Maddox for you losing Betty?"

"Yes," he hissed out. "If she hadn't gotten pregnant, I might have had a chance." His anger was back.

"But Maddox is innocent in all this. He didn't ask to be conceived."

"I know that," he spit at me. "I tried to be reasonable," he said, his voice calmer now. "But, every time I see him"—he clenched his fists—"it makes my blood boil. These last twelve years were the first peace I'd had after eighteen years."

"But seeing Betty doesn't bother you?"

He gave me a look.

"Sorry." The question had just flown out of my mouth.

Human behavior was weird. He should have been blaming Betty or maybe even himself. He might have read more into their relationship than there really had been. But he was the type of guy who would never see his own faults. And Betty was his love. He couldn't or wouldn't be mad at her. So, poor Maddox got the full brunt of Sheriff Whitlock's anger.

"Did you ever talk to someone about it?"

He looked at me like an alien was growing out of my head. "I don't do any of that New Age bullshit."

"No, of course not." I rolled my eyes. "Did you break into Maddox's apartment and steal his gun?"

"*No*. I'm still the sheriff."

I held up my hands. "Okay, okay. I was just checking."

"I know what you think of me," he said.

I gave him the once-over. "I highly doubt that."

"You think I'm a bitter, old fool."

"I think you're a bitter man who needs to stop repressing your feelings because it turns you into an asshole. And you need better friends," I said as everyone in the interrogation room stood. "My father doesn't care about anyone but himself."

I left the adjoining room and met them in the hall. The detective nodded at me as he walked past.

"How'd it go?" I asked Olivia.

"Good, I think. I think the detective believes him. It's just the gun that's a big red flag. Hopefully, whoever stole the gun left fingerprints."

No one said it, but we also hoped Brandon would wake up and tell us who'd shot him.

44

MADDOX

I waited at baggage claim for Flash to get off his plane. It was two days after my arrest, and even though I'd told Flash it would be a few months before I went to trial, he'd insisted on coming.

I was hoping the charges would be dropped altogether, and there would be no trial. No one but Addison was able to alibi me. And wouldn't you know it? The PI her dad had hired had already gone home for the night. I guessed the guy needed to sleep, too, but it was just my luck. He had been there to take pictures of me having sex but not when I needed to get out of an attempted murder conviction.

"Mad Dog."

I spun around from where I had been picking up my coffee to see Flash cupping his mouth from bellowing my name.

A grin split across my face. I hadn't realized how much I'd missed him until I saw him again.

When we reached each other, we locked hands and pulled each other into a back-slapping hug.

"Dude, it seems I have to come and help your ass out when you're in trouble, even when you're retired."

"Fuck off," I said with a laugh. "Thanks for coming."

"Mad Dog."

I looked around to see who else would be yelling my name across the terminal.

Evan was coming out of the restroom and making a beeline for Flash and me.

I looked at Flash. He hadn't said anything about Evan coming.

He shrugged. "He made me bring him."

"How'd you both manage leave?"

"Begged and pleaded. And Evan had to suck the CO's dick, but we're here."

"Fuck you, asshole," Evan said as he reached us. "You're just jealous that I'm not sucking yours."

Flash lifted his middle finger and pushed it in Evan's face. Evan pushed him away and punched him in the side.

Damn. I'd missed these guys.

"Ladies, it's too early to fight. Can we save this for later?"

This got me a, "Screw you," from both of them.

I just laughed.

A few seconds later, the baggage chute started up, and luggage began falling out. Flash and Evan grabbed their duffel bags, and we headed to my SUV.

"How's the case going?" Flash asked from the passenger seat.

"It's only been two days," I pointed out.

"Yeah, but they have to be making some progress."

"I can tell you that the detective in charge is doing a lot better job than the county sheriff. He's former military. We have a certain understanding."

"Navy?" Evan asked.

"Marines."

"Fucking jarhead," Flash said as he shook his head.

"Did he question your future father-in-law?" Evan asked

Father-in-law?

"I told him about Addison," Flash said, reading my mind.

"I believe he's been questioned, yes, but I haven't exactly been let into the loop of the investigation." I sighed. "Let's talk about something else. What have I missed since I've been gone?"

We got to Brook Creek around seven in the morning. It was a Wednesday, so people were heading off to work, but it still wasn't very busy.

"Holy shit, you really do live in BFE," Flash said. He'd grown up in New York and not realized places like this even existed outside of television.

"Man, and I thought Afghanistan was bad," Evan said from the backseat. "You actually *choose* to live here?"

"Yes, dickhead, I do."

Ice was from Phoenix and didn't understand small-town life any more than Flash did.

Although I didn't understand it too much either at the moment. Everyone was avoiding me, except for Addison and my family. Even people I'd thought I was on good terms with, like Dani, wouldn't look me in the eye. Foster had even asked me not to come to work until things settled down some. My old teammates coming into town was a welcome distraction.

We pulled around the back of my apartment building and

exited my vehicle. I opened the back of the SUV, so the guys could get their stuff before I led them inside.

They dropped their bags on the floor with a thud and sat down on my couch.

I took a seat on the end of the armrest. "You two can stay here, and I'll stay next door at Addison's. You're going to have to flip for who gets the bed and who gets the couch."

The two of them immediately put their hands in Rock-Paper-Scissors position.

"One time. Winner takes the bedroom," Flash said.

"Agreed."

"One, two, three," they said at the same time.

"Ha! Yes," Flash said. "Scissors cuts paper."

"Best two of three."

"No way. I won. You're sleeping on the couch."

"Maddox?"

The three of them turned to see my beautiful, naked girlfriend standing in the doorway of my bedroom. I hadn't realized she was still there because the door was open when we got there.

Her dark hair was messed up from sleep and from me fucking her good-bye that morning, and she was rubbing her eyes, so she had no clue we could all see her.

Her nipples were berry red from my mouth and erect from the cool air hitting them. And, to top it off, she had two sets of pink fingerprints on her hips from where I'd gripped her waist as I took her from behind before I left.

"I thought I heard voices," she said.

"Shit." I jumped out of my spot on the sofa, directly in front of her, and blocked my friends from seeing any more than they already had. "Addy, remember how I told you my old teammates were coming, and I had to pick them up this morning?"

She dropped her hands from her face, her eyebrows furrowed. Realization slowly dawned in her sleepy eyes. "Oh, yeah. Are they here?"

I looked behind me. Both men sat on the edge of the couch with their mouths hanging open.

I turned back to her. "Yeah, baby." I raised my eyebrows. "They're here." I kissed her. "Why don't you go get dressed? Then, you can come out and say hi."

Once she fully woke up, she was going to be embarrassed, but right now, she simply shrugged. "Okay."

I put my hands on her shoulders and spun her around. I nudged her into the bedroom. "Get dressed." And then I shut the door behind her.

I could only imagine what my friends had to say to me. I swung around, waiting for their wisecracks.

"Damn, man. No wonder you were like, *See ya, Stephanie,*" Evan said.

"Holy *fuck*, Mad Dog. I see why you hopped into her bed right after you got back to town. History or no history."

I walked toward the kitchen, smacking each of them on the back of their head. "That's mine, assholes. No touching. I don't share."

45

ADDISON

I woke up, facedown, on Maddox's bed, groggy from sleep. I rolled onto my back, waiting for my brain to catch up with my body. I hadn't slept very well the last few nights since Maddox's arrest, and I missed waking up, refreshed.

I might need to invest in some sleeping pills if this didn't get better.

I sat up, taking my time. I was naked, and I searched for yesterday's clothes. They were in a pile at the bottom of the bed on the floor, so I snatched them up and got dressed.

Putting on my top and shorts triggered a dream I'd had that morning. I knew it was morning because Maddox had kissed me good-bye, and then I'd gotten up to use the bathroom before falling back asleep.

I had dreamed that Maddox had come home with his friends, and I'd walked out of the bedroom, naked as the day I had been born.

Yikes.

What a way to welcome Maddox's guests. Sometimes, morning dreams were the worst ones and definitely the most vivid.

I looked at the clock. *Crap*. It was already eight o'clock.

I'd slept longer than I'd wanted to. But I'd needed the rest, so I couldn't complain too much. Plus, my first appointment wasn't until nine thirty.

I opened the bedroom door to the smell of bacon and coffee. Now, those two things would help start my morning right.

I stopped in the bathroom to brush my hair and use the toilet again. When I walked into the kitchen, Maddox was drying and putting away a skillet, and two guys I'd never seen before stared at me.

They almost looked scared, which I thought was weird. I thought Navy SEALs weren't afraid of anything. Maybe I should have put on some makeup. I didn't think I looked that bad though.

"I left you some bacon." Maddox pointed to a small plate and warily eyed me, too. "You okay, Addy?"

"Uh, yeah, I'm fine. Just tired." I took a mug from the cupboard and poured myself some coffee. I turned and put my back against the counter. "Are you going to introduce me?"

He smiled, but it was kind of a laugh. "Sure." He pointed to the bigger of the two. "This is Senior Chief Thomas 'Flash' Morelli."

I held out my palm. "Hi."

He stood from his seat at the island and stuck out his giant paw. He was about an inch or two taller than Maddox and had more muscles, which surprised me because I thought Maddox was pretty damn muscular. He had dark brown hair and deep brown eyes. He kind of reminded me of a teddy bear. A sexy teddy bear.

"What do I call you?" I asked.

He grinned. "Mad Dog calls me Flash, but you can just call me Tommy, ma'am."

I smiled back. "Okay, Tommy. And you can call me Addison. I threatened to sue the last man who'd called me ma'am." I winked at him.

Tommy looked at Maddox and widened his eyes, but he looked amused.

"And this is Petty Officer Evan 'Ice' Malone."

This friend was a couple of inches shorter than Maddox and thinner, but I could tell he had his own set of muscles under his T-shirt. His hair was a lighter brown, his eyes were blue, and he looked like he was about seventeen. I was sure he was quite a bit older, or he wouldn't be a Navy SEAL. I also didn't doubt that he had his own share of women. He had a *golly, gee whiz* kind of look about him that he probably totally played up with the ladies.

He shook my hand as well. "You can call me Evan."

I looked at Maddox. "What was your rank?" Not that I knew what any of it meant.

"I was a chief petty officer when I retired."

"And they call you Mad Dog?"

He smiled. "Yep."

"How did you get your nicknames?"

Maddox shrugged. "Mine is just because of my name. Maddox equals Mad, and Wolfe equals Dog. Because it's such a common nickname, the minute my first team heard my name, they nicknamed me Mad Dog."

"And Flash?"

"It's because everyone underestimates my size," he said. "I'm faster than I look."

Maddox and Evan snickered, and I figured there was more to that story.

"My nickname is because I'm smooth as ice," Evan said.

Flash laughed and pounded his fist in front of him. "You wish. It's because Mr. Arizona here fell down about twenty times his first winter in Virginia. It doesn't even get that bad there. You need to come to New York in winter."

Evan shuddered. "No, thank you. Besides, your nickname is because you make the ladies scatter in a flash." Evan was clearly trying to get back at Tommy for embarrassing him, but it didn't work.

Tommy laughed and took a sip of his coffee. "Yeah, I know."

Evan and Maddox looked surprised.

"You do?" Evan said.

Tommy grinned like he had something great to say. He leaned toward Evan. "But women don't run away from me for the reason you think."

"Oh, really?" Evan said, his face and voice full of doubt.

"Yeah. See, I'm not stupid, and I asked a group of women once. Believe it or not, because I'm a big guy, they worry I'm a *big* guy. They're afraid I'll hurt them or something."

Evan's eyebrows furrowed in confusion, and Tommy looked at me. He obviously wanted to explain it to his friend, but he didn't want to say anything in front of me.

I didn't know if it was because I was a woman, a stranger, or both, but I rolled my eyes. "He's saying he's got a big dick, Evan. So big that women are afraid to have sex with him."

Tommy barked out a laugh, and Evan turned red.

"God, I love it when a woman says *dick*." Tommy drained his coffee and shrugged. "Or *cock*. There's something about a naughty word coming out of a pretty mouth." He set his mug down with a thump. "You have a gas station around here?"

"Yeah, it's just a few blocks away."

"Great." Tommy got up from his seat. "I'll be back in a half hour."

Evan drank down the rest of his coffee, too, and scrambled off his seat. "I'm coming with."

The apartment door slammed, and I turned to pick up my plate of bacon. I carried it to the spot Evan had just vacated.

"Your friends are fun." I picked up a slice of bacon and took a big bite.

Maddox leaned over and rested his arms on the counter. "They kind of thought the same thing about you."

I tilted my head to the side. "But they just met me. When did they tell you that?"

He laughed. "You must have fallen back asleep."

"Huh?"

"After I got home, you woke up."

I still wasn't following.

"I sent you back to the room and told you to get dressed. But you must have lain down and gone back to sleep because you didn't come out until an hour later."

My bacon dropped from my hand. "Ah, *hell*. It wasn't a dream, was it?"

His friends had totally seen me naked.

Maddox picked up my bacon and popped it in his mouth. "No, babe, it wasn't." He pulled my head forward by the back of my neck and kissed me. "But don't worry. I told them this"—he gestured from my head to my feet—"is all mine, and if they touch you, they die."

The corner of my mouth tilted up. "Yours, huh?"

"I think we established you were mine the night I snuck into your room, and you spread your legs for me."

I wrinkled my nose.

Damn him.

He was right.

46

MADDOX

I lifted my tired lids and looked up at Addison's dark ceiling. It was still night, yet something had woken me. I'd been in the military long enough to know when I woke on my own and when something had roused me from slumber.

My phone started vibrating next to me on Addison's nightstand. I picked it up and frowned at the number. I didn't recognize it.

"Hello?" I answered in a whisper, so I wouldn't wake Addison.

"Maddox," a shaky voice on the other end said.

It took me a couple seconds to realize who it was.

"Ben?"

What the hell was a kid doing, calling me in the middle of the night? When he'd asked me for my number the day Addison and I visited him, I didn't think he'd ever use it.

"Yeah."

I gently rolled Addison away from my side and sat up. "What's wrong?"

"My-my-my dad."

"What about him?"

"He's here. And I think he's hurting my mom."

As if I needed proof, there was a distant cry from the other side of the line.

Shit.

"Okay, Ben, listen to me. Are you able to get out of the house without your dad seeing you?"

"I-I don't think so."

That didn't surprise me. The house was small.

"Okay then, can you get to the bathroom?"

"I think so."

"Okay, go there and lock the door. Keep the phone with you. I'll be there as soon as I can."

As I threw on my clothes as fast as I could, I called Flash. My friends had picked the perfect time to come to town. And, after two days of being bored, they wouldn't be able to complain about not having some excitement.

"Yeah?" Flash answered.

"Meet me outside. I need some help with a domestic situation."

"On it."

In the Navy, Flash had ranked over me since he was an officer, and I was enlisted. I wasn't in the military anymore, but I would probably always see him as my superior. Yet he was also my friend, and he knew I wouldn't tell him to do something if it wasn't important.

I hung up, kissed Addison good-bye, and slipped out the door.

One minute later, Flash and Evan showed up.

Everyone piled into my SUV, and I explained the situation to the guys as I drove.

"Shouldn't we be calling the police?"

"No police station, remember? We're too small. We just have the sheriff's department. That's why I told Ben to call me if he ever had any trouble. I didn't think he'd ever need my number though."

"Are you saying the sheriff is so bad that he wouldn't help a woman getting beat by her ex-husband?" Evan asked.

"God, I hope not. But let's not take the chance of finding out."

When we got close to Claire's home, I parked down the street. I didn't want this guy running away. After what he was putting Claire and Ben through, I wanted him to go to jail for a bit.

We climbed out and looked around.

"I sure wish I had my gun on me," Flash said.

"Me, too." The state police had taken all my weapons to test them. "We're going to have to go into this with just our fists."

Flash cracked his knuckles. "It's a good thing I have huge fists."

I laughed. "Let's go."

"Is this guy big?" Evan asked me.

"Not from what I remember, but I haven't seen him for over twelve years." When we got close, I said, "Why don't you guys take the perimeter, and the back door, while I go knock on the front? I'm already in enough trouble. Maybe I can talk this guy down."

Flash and Evan nodded and then split up. One went to the west side of the house, and the other went to the east. I went to the south side and knocked on the door.

I could hear yelling inside, but no one answered, so I knocked louder.

The door swung open.

"What the fuck do you want?" Mickey Williams said from the other side of the threshold.

I barely recognized him. He looked about twenty years older instead of twelve, and he had a massive beer gut.

"Where's Claire?"

"Busy."

Yeah, right.

I stepped into the house and pushed Mickey out of the way. I turned, so he'd be in my peripheral vision. I didn't need him getting the drop on me.

"Claire?"

No answer.

I stepped further into the house. "Claire?" I called again just as Flash and Evan came through the back door. Knowing they would take care of Mickey, I concentrated on finding his victim. "Claire, it's Maddox. Addison's friend."

I heard movement in the kitchen, and I slowly walked that way. When I rounded the counter, I was unprepared for what I saw.

I'd been overseas, fighting in some grizzly shit, but seeing a woman lying on the floor of her own kitchen, covered in blood, made me want to puke. Her pants were around her ankles, and she was cradling an arm that was bent in the wrong spot.

I turned and looked at Mickey. "You sick fuck."

He roared out his rage and made a beeline for me. He didn't get far though because Flash and Evan pulled him back. Mickey went flying, landing on his back.

I took out my phone and called 911. Claire needed medical attention, and Mickey needed to get his ass arrested.

After giving the dispatcher the address, I hung up. She'd wanted me to stay on the line, but I didn't have time for that.

I tucked my phone in my pocket and knelt next to Claire. I brushed my hands over her hair. "Hey, Claire?"

One eye blinked open because the other was swollen shut, and she looked scared for a moment.

"Hey. It's me, Maddox." I held up my hands, so she could see them. "I'm here to help."

She tried to look around, which was hard with one eye black and blue and inflamed.

"Don't worry. My two friends have Mickey under control in the other room. He's not going to hurt you."

"B-Ben."

"Yeah, I'm going to go check on him. He's the one who called me. I told him to hide in the bathroom and lock the door."

Her eye closed. "Thank you."

I stood and went in search of a blanket. I couldn't let her just lie on the floor with her pants down. I couldn't find one, so I took the comforter from her bed and brought it back to the kitchen to put over her.

Then, I went in search of Ben.

I knocked on the bathroom door. "Hey, Ben. It's Maddox. You can come out now."

I heard the lock click, and the door opened a crack. I waved at Ben. Then, he flung it open, threw himself into my arms, and started to cry.

47

ADDISON

Olivia threw her legs up onto my desk and crossed them at the ankles. "Holy shit. I couldn't have asked for better PR." She turned her laptop and showed me her screen.

A former Navy SEAL, who's been accused of attempted murder, came to the rescue of a woman and her young son last night.

She turned the computer back, so she could see it and lowered the volume. "He's made the news. All the way in Des Moines."

Yeah, it was great for Maddox's reputation, but…

"You know there is a woman in the hospital with a broken arm, a broken eye socket, and three cracked ribs, who was raped, right?" I now had two people I had to visit in the hospital, and it was hard because the hospital was an hour away.

Olivia sighed. "I know. And I feel sorry for Clara."

"Claire," I corrected.

She waved my comment away. "Claire. Whatever. But it's

not like Maddox made her ex come back and beat her. We might as well enjoy the publicity."

I shook my head. "I could never be a defense attorney." Ironic since Maddox not having a good defense attorney twelve years ago was the reason I had gone into law. Now, I was happy with writing wills, working on estates, and handling the occasional misdemeanor. Felonies were something I didn't want to be involved in, especially high-profile ones.

"When is Maddox going to get here anyway?"

"He and the guys went back to sleep for a bit. I told Maddox I'd hold you off for a while."

She mock laughed. "You're so funny."

"Seriously though. He went there at about one in the morning, and by the time the sheriff and state police came and took their statements, it was about four a.m. They were tired."

"Well, I hope he gets here soon. I have to be back in Des Moines for an appointment this afternoon."

Just then, the front door opened, and Maddox walked in with Tommy and Evan. I watched them through the open door of my office.

"Hey, Serena," Maddox said.

"Hey, Uncle Maddox."

"Guys, this is my niece, Serena."

"Hi," she said.

"Serena, this is Tommy, and this is Evan. I used to work with them."

They both smiled at her.

"Nice to meet you," Evan said.

Maddox pointed to his friends, moving his finger from

one friend to the other. "The rules that apply to Addison also apply to her." He pointed at Serena. "Hands off."

Olivia made a noise, and I looked over at her.

"Please tell me I'm not representing some caveman," she said in a low voice.

I laughed. "Don't knock it till you try it," I whispered back. "Maddox would never boss me around…except in the bedroom." I wiggled my eyebrows. "There's something hot about being dragged off to the cave by your hair and being taken from behind."

She looked at me like I was crazy. "No, thank you. I'll stick to nice, respectable men who treat me like a lady."

"Your orgasms must suck," Flash said from behind her, "and be super boring."

I had just taken a sip of my coffee, and I about spit it out from laughter when I watched Olivia jump in her seat.

She dropped her feet, turned around in her chair, and glared at him, her brown eyes narrowed in anger.

He shrugged. "If you even have any at all. *Excuse me, miss. I'd like to make you come now,*" he said in a voice slightly higher than his own. "*Okay, but be careful. I can't ruin my hair or my makeup,*" Flash said, pretending to be Olivia.

"You don't even know me."

Flash laughed. "I've met your kind before. Big and bad to the world, but behind closed doors, you need your ass slapped and your pussy pounded."

Olivia gasped, and I bit my lip to keep from laughing. This was a different side of Flash than I'd seen the morning I met him.

"Flash," Maddox said, coming into the room, "leave my lawyer alone. I want her to defend me, not run away, cursing my name because of my friends." He stepped around his friend. "Please don't throw my trial because of one asshole."

Olivia patted Maddox's hand. "Don't worry. I've dealt with worse men than him before." She looked at Tommy. "Nice name," she said sarcastically.

He snickered. "It's a nickname, sweetheart." He raised his eyebrows. "You can ask Addison about it later."

She threw her hair over her shoulder. "I don't think so."

Tommy shrugged. "Like I said, boring." He laid his head on his shoulder and pretended to snore.

Maddox socked him in the gut. "Knock it off, asswipe." Then, he walked over to my chair and lifted me out of my seat.

I squealed.

He sat down in my chair and settled me on his lap. "So, what do you want to go over today?" Maddox asked and nuzzled my neck.

Evan walked into my office as Olivia said, "Well, first, congratulations are in order for what happened early this morning. This will look very good to any potential jury."

Tommy scowled. "Mad Dog didn't do it for the publicity. We did it because someone was in trouble."

Olivia rolled her eyes. "I know that. But it helps our case nonetheless."

"She's kind of right," Evan said. "Everyone was waiting to shake Mad Dog's hand when we went to get breakfast this morning. Ours, too. But they were looking at Mad Dog like he was a hero."

I looked at Maddox, and he scowled.

"Everyone likes me now, I guess. Me being me wasn't good enough," he said the last sentence for my ears only.

I kissed him on the cheek. "You don't need them."

Olivia went over a few more things with Maddox, and then the guys took off.

I went through some of my paperwork while Olivia typed away, but I noticed she kept giving me side-eyed glances.

"Ask me," I said, not looking up from my desk.

"What?"

I lifted my head. "I know you want to know, Olivia. Ask me."

She rolled her eyes. "How did Flash get his nickname? And what is his real name? I wasn't actually introduced."

"His name is Tommy. And he got the nickname because he said the ladies are gone in a flash when they go out to the bar."

"I can see why." She furrowed her brows. "He made it sound like his nickname was a good thing."

"Well, apparently, the women avoid him because they're afraid of his size."

"He is a big guy. But I didn't get the impression he'd hurt anyone."

I laughed. "No, not his body size. The size of his dick."

Olivia's cheeks turned pink. I didn't think I'd ever seen her blush before.

"Oh," she said as she fingered the corner of her laptop. "That never occurred to me."

I chuckled. "Maybe Tommy is right, and you've been with the wrong guys. You haven't had sex until you've had sex with someone with a big cock."

Her eyes widened. "Does Maddox…"

"Hell yeah. Why do you think I can't keep my hands off him? It's big, and he knows what to do with it."

"I've never had that."

I grinned. "I'm sure Flash would be more than happy to show you."

Her spine stiffened. "No, thank you."

I gave her a once-over, taking in her small frame. "You're probably right. He might break you in two."

48

MADDOX

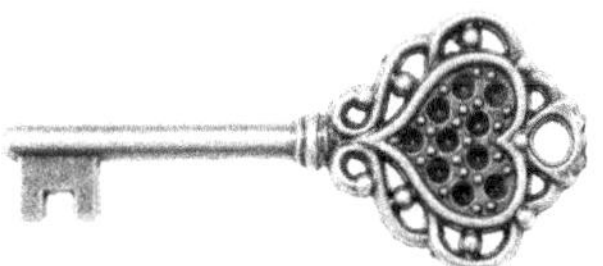

Addison kissed her way down my chest and my stomach. She looked up at me from her position between my legs and grinned.

I slightly lifted my hips off the bed to show her what I wanted. Not that she didn't already know.

She gripped my cock in her hand and placed gentle kisses on my pelvis, then the base of my cock, and up until she reached the tip. It was like she was making love to my dick with her mouth, but at the same time, it was agony.

Holding my shaft in her fist, she looked me in the eyes as she swirled her tongue around my tip before she finally sucked me into her mouth. But just my head.

I groaned. She smiled the best she could with her mouth shaped like an O.

I'd agreed to let her do what she wanted to me, but this was beginning to feel like torture.

I slid my hand around the back of her neck and into her hair. Giving a small tug, I said, "Suck me in all the way, Addy. I want to feel your mouth around me."

She'd been lying on the bed, but she got up on her knees. And back, back, back my cock went into her mouth. God, I loved it when she deep-throated me. My shaft was in her throat now, and I could feel it tighten around me as she struggled to keep me there. It felt incredible, but her eyes were watering, so I pulled her head back off me.

I rubbed the back of her neck. "You know, you don't have to do that if you don't like it."

My dick was screaming, *Shut up, asshole,* but I ignored him.

She grinned and wiped the tears from her eyes. "I like doing it. I wish I could do it more and for longer." She crawled up my body and kissed me. "I love making you feel good."

I rolled her onto her back. "Same here." I lifted her leg and pushed inside her.

Her neck bowed, and her back arched.

I didn't think I'd ever get sick of seeing that reaction from her. Just from my cock being inside her. I could admit, it made me feel pretty fucking powerful.

I kissed her neck and shoulder as I thrust inside her. I licked my first two fingers of one hand and wrapped my arm around her.

Pushing my hand under her butt, I spread her cheeks and rubbed a finger around her sweet little butthole. I had learned that one of Addison's favorite things was double stimulation.

I pushed one digit inside her tight hole.

She moaned and dug her nails into my sides.

"You like that, don't you, baby?"

Her eyes tightly shut, and she nodded.

"Do you ever wonder what it would be like to have two cocks in you?"

Her answer was to suck in her breath.

I chuckled. "Yeah, you've thought about it." I pushed my finger in further and began fucking her ass with it. I lowered my mouth to her ear. "I hate to break it to you, baby, but no one is touching you as long as you're with me. You're mine, and I don't share."

Rather unexpectedly, Addison exploded in my arms. Her pussy tightened around my cock and her ass around my fingers.

Usually, I could tell when she was getting close, but this one caught me by surprise.

After her orgasm waned, I slowly slipped my hand from her behind.

She blinked up at me.

"Weren't expecting that, huh?"

She shook her head. "No."

"Do you like it when I tell you that you're mine?"

She nodded, looking embarrassed. "I probably shouldn't."

I frowned, pushing myself deeper inside her. "Why?"

She smiled. "Because I'm supposed to be an independent woman. No man owns me. That sort of thing."

I laughed. "I won't tell anyone." I kissed her. "And, if it helps, I'm yours."

She brought my head back down and kissed me again. "Good." She lifted her legs and wrapped them around my waist. "Now, come inside me and show me I'm yours."

I took her hands in mine and raised them over her head.

I began thrusting again. I hadn't been close before

Addison came, but I could feel myself reaching my climax rather quickly. "Tell me you're mine, Addison."

"I'm yours, Maddox."

"Again."

"I'm yours." She squeezed my fingers and lifted her hips. "I love you."

I pounded into Addison's body now, my mind chanting her words over and over in my head. My balls tightened, and my spine tingled. With one last hard thrust, I drove inside her as far as I could and let myself go.

My breathing erratic, I released her hands and collapsed on top of her.

She rubbed her hands up and down my back, soothing me with her caresses.

"I love you, too," I told her. I rolled off her, so I didn't suffocate her with my weight. I put my arm under her head and pulled her to my chest. "I hope I die while making love to you."

"Yeah, that'd be good for you, but I'm not into necrophilia."

I laughed.

She ran her hands on my chest. "Hopefully, we'll be so old when we pass that we won't even be thinking of sex anymore."

I raised my eyebrows. "Speak for yourself. I'm still going to be fucking you when we're ninety."

She smiled, but there was sadness behind her eyes.

"What's wrong?"

"What if they take you away from me, Maddox? I don't know if I can bear to lose you again."

I turned to my side and pulled her close. "We're going to

fight like hell, so that doesn't happen. I'm not too fond of being taken away either."

"Gah. I sound so selfish," she said into my chest. "You'd be the one going to prison. At least I'd be free."

I rubbed her back. "It's okay, Addy. I know what you meant." I held her tight to me. I hoped that we'd get many more nights like this.

"I keep hoping for a miracle."

"I do, too, baby. I do, too."

49

ADDISON

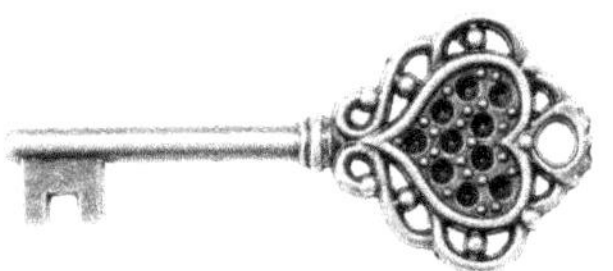

A miracle did come. Saturday morning, I was helping Maddox clean his apartment. He'd taken his friends to the airport last night, and we were left with the mess they'd made.

"Your friends are pigs."

There were pizza boxes and beer bottles lined up. And the bathroom…I'd told Maddox I loved him but not that much. The bathroom was all his.

Maddox shrugged. "They're guys."

"You're not a pig," I pointed out.

"That's because I have to live here. They aren't like this back home either." He looked around. "Well, not this bad anyway."

I'd just picked up the last empty bottle when Maddox's cell phone rang. I threw the bottle in the recycling as he took his phone from his back pocket.

"I don't recognize the number," he said.

"Put it on speaker."

He swiped to answer. "Hello?"

"Maddox?"

"This is he."

"This is Detective Porter."

Maddox and I met each other's eyes.

"What can I do for you?" Maddox asked.

"I need you to come down to the station. I have some more questions for you."

I had no idea what this meant. Detective Porter had a voice I couldn't read. It was probably one of the things that made him a good detective. He didn't give anything away.

I nodded to Maddox.

"I'll be there in about a half hour. I need to call my lawyer and have her meet me there."

"See you then."

Maddox hit End on his phone and looked at me again.

"I'll call Olivia," I said.

Maddox and I walked into the station a half hour later.

When I'd called Olivia, she'd chewed me out for not giving her more of a head start. I'd told her I could handle things until then. I might not be a trial lawyer, but I wasn't going to let my boyfriend say anything stupid.

Once inside, Sheriff Whitlock didn't take me and Maddox to the interrogation room. Instead, we were both directed toward a different area that said *Conference Room*.

"What is going on, Sheriff?"

He held up his hands. "I don't know, missy. Since I was taken off the case, they've been doing things without me. I'm not privy to this little meeting," he said with narrowed eyes.

"Hey, *I* didn't call in the state police." Only because I hadn't thought of it.

He opened the door. "Just get in there."

When we walked in, I was surprised to see my father and Simon standing in the room. Detective Porter was also there, sitting in the corner, looking over some paperwork.

The sheriff closed the door from the other side.

"My daughter is finally present. Can you please tell me why you called us all here?" my father said impatiently.

The detective rose from his seat and shot a look at my father. He immediately stepped back, and I had to disguise my laughter with a cough.

"I have some news," Porter said. "Brandon Taylor is awake."

I clapped my hands over my mouth as a tear slipped down my face. I dropped my hands as Maddox pulled me into his arms and kissed my head.

"Please tell me he's going to be okay."

"I don't have all the news, miss, but it looks like he's getting better."

"Thank God," I said. I looked at Maddox and gasped. I turned back to the detective. "Does this mean he told you who really shot him?"

He looked disappointed, and my hopes fell. "That's why I wanted you all here."

My father's chin lifted. "Why me? Why Simon? We don't have anything to do with this case."

"Because I have a question for you."

"What?" My father sounded like his time couldn't be wasted any more than it already had been. He was so rude.

"Who inherits your fortune and all your businesses if you die?"

"Addison, of course."

"But is it true that you've made hints that Mr. Deavor would inherit them if he married your daughter?"

My father looked guilty. "Perhaps things of that nature have been said. It's not a secret that I've been hoping Addison would take an interest in Simon," he said defensively.

"But then you've also insisted that Brandon Taylor head up your current project because he and your daughter had a romantic history?"

My father's spine straightened. "I just wanted to get her away from the Wolfe boy."

"*Dad*, how could you?"

My father pointed at him. "You can do better than him."

I was ready to yell at him, but Maddox said, "He's not worth it."

"What does any of this have to do with Brandon Taylor?"

"I was making sure that you didn't set up Mr. Wolfe for the murder of Mr. Taylor."

My father sputtered, "What-what-what—I would never do something that despicable."

No, he would just spy on me, try to bribe my boyfriend, and send someone innocent to prison.

Asshole.

Detective Porter nodded. "I really didn't think it was you. Besides, Mr. Taylor already told us who tried to kill him."

I gasped.

"Then, why are you asking me all these questions?" my father asked, outraged.

"Because I had to make sure you weren't the one behind your assistant trying to commit murder."

My father took a step away from his protégé. "Simon?"

Simon was as white as my bathtub.

"I also wanted to see all four of your reactions when you found out that Mr. Taylor was alive. Mr. Deavor, you are the only one who looks like you are going to shit a brick."

"Fuck all of you," Simon said, exploding. "Fuck you for leading me on like I might have a chance at inheriting your business," he said to my father. "Fuck you for not just marrying me when it's what your father wants," he said to me. "Fuck you for coming back here and not staying away. I would have worn her down eventually," he said to Maddox.

"Yes, because that's the kind of girl you want. One who barely tolerates you."

"Fuck you."

"You already said that," Maddox said with a bored expression.

"Well then, fuck you," he said to Porter, "for figuring it out. I was so close to getting rid of Maddox and Brandon. I have waited on this man hand and foot"—he pointed to my father—"and done everything he asked for. And, when his daughter pretty much walked out of his life, you know what he said to me?"

No one answered.

"He said, 'Thanks, but I can't leave anything to you when I pass.' I've bent over backward while you two hate each other." He pointed to me. "And you're still getting everything when he dies. He couldn't even leave me one little part."

Detective Porter took out his handcuffs and swung Simon around. "You have the right to remain silent..."

50

MADDOX

I listened to Detective Porter read Simon Deavor his rights. I was trying to pretend like his confession didn't bother me. But I barely knew the guy, and he had set me up for murder. He had been willing to take someone's *life*.

All because he wanted Addison's father's money.

As the detective was leading Simon out the door, he turned to me. "I'll contact the DA to drop all charges against you as soon as I can."

I nodded. "Thank you."

And then it was just Addison, her father, and me in the room.

Brantley cleared his throat. "I apologize for my assistant," he said to me. "I had no idea he would do something like this."

"Maybe you should be more careful about who you hire. And who you select to marry your daughter."

"Addison," her father warned.

"No, Dad. You might not have committed murder or

attempted murder, but you tried to buy Maddox out of my life. You're not that much better." She marched up to him. "And I know Maddox's lawyer asked me to testify twelve years ago. You never told me."

Her father blanched and started stuttering, "I-I—"

"Don't even bother lying at this point. Maddox's lawyer has the attorney's notes from his first conviction. There was a copy of the letter in the files." A tear fell from her eyes. "You were willing to let an innocent man go to prison for something he didn't do just to get him out of my life."

"He's hardly innocent." Brantley seemed to have regained his voice. "I know what you two were doing that night and why you were able to alibi him."

Addison rolled her eyes. "So what? Teenagers having sex is not a criminal offense. And Maddox was not guilty of the robbery."

"I—"

"I don't care," she cut him off. "I don't want you in my life, I don't want your money, and I don't need your blessing. Just stay away from me."

I took her hand. "Come on, Addy. Let's go."

With a slight tug on my part, she came with me out the door. I took her around the corner and pulled her into my arms to let her cry.

"Oh my God, what happened?" Olivia yelled as she made a beeline for us.

"No, Olivia, it's not—"

"Why didn't you wait for me?" She pulled out her phone and began pacing back and forth.

"Olivia."

She was shaking her head back and forth. "This is what happens when clients don't listen to me."

"Olivia, shut up," Addison said from my chest.

Olivia froze as her eyes widened.

"Will you just listen to Maddox, please?"

I bit the inside of my cheek to not laugh at the two women.

Olivia looked at me with raised eyebrows.

"They found out that Simon had done it," I told her. "Brandon woke up this morning and told them it wasn't me."

"And Simon just confessed," Addison mumbled.

Olivia clapped her hands. "Yes. Victory." She pointed at me. "I'm still billing you for the hours."

"Okay," I said as Addison said, "No way."

Olivia backed up, so she could look from the corner we'd just come around. "Do you think Simon has an attorney?"

Addison lifted her head. "If you represent him, I'll cut you."

Olivia rolled her eyes and held her hands up in surrender. "Fine, fine."

"You don't want to be his lawyer anyway," I told her. "He confessed, and the victim can identify him."

She smirked at me. "But I do love a challenge."

Yikes. I bet she did.

She looked at Addison. "But I'll stay away from him. Out of respect for our friendship." She raised her phone and began typing away on it.

Addison put her hand on her hip. "Then, what are you doing?"

"I'm contacting the media. We need to do a press conference."

"No," I said.

She sighed and looked at me. "An interview then?"

I hesitated.

"I'll waive my fee," she said in a singsong voice.

"Five-minute interview. Not a second more."

She grinned.

"And no talking about my time in the service, or the interview is over."

Olivia frowned and lowered her phone. "But that's one of the things they'll want to talk about."

"I'll answer basic questions but nothing about what I did while overseas."

She sighed. "Fine."

"And I'm not dressing up. You can take me as I am."

She looked horrified. "But…you're wearing cargo pants."

"Fatigues," I corrected.

"Tomayto, tomahto. They look the same."

I shrugged. "Take it or leave it."

"Fine," she said as she turned around and put her phone to her ear.

"Ooh, my man is going to be famous," Addison teased.

I frowned at her. I didn't want to be famous. Not even a little bit.

She tapped her chin. "Of course, then everyone's going to see how hot you are, and you'll be getting letters and used panties in the mail."

I wrinkled my nose. *No, thank you.*

She gasped and grinned. "I know. I'm going to write *Addison's Man* on you. We'll put *Addison* on your forehead, and then the *M* on your left cheek, an *A* on your nose, and the *N* on the right cheek."

She outlined her plan on my face with her finger as she said it, and I shook her hand away.

"I don't think so."

She blew a raspberry at me. "You're no fun."

I wiggled my left hand. "Why don't you just put a ring on it?"

Her eyes widened. "I'm going to pretend like you didn't just say that because that is not how you're going to propose to me."

"Why not?" I teased.

"The sheriff's department. Really? And you don't even have a ring."

"Well, it is where we met up again after twelve years."

"*No,*" she said and turned her back to me and walked away.

I laughed as I followed her out.

51

ADDISON

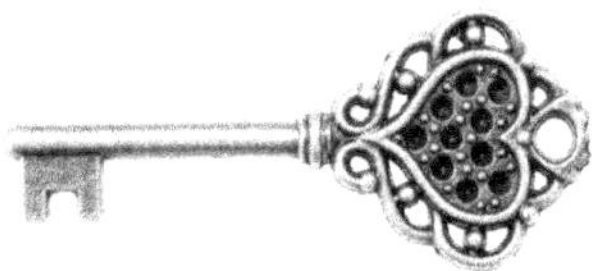

There were several groups of townspeople crowded outside as Maddox prepped with the reporter and Olivia. He'd opted to have the interview on the edge of town, next to the sign that said *Brook Creek*. Word had spread like wildfire about the interview, and people were coming in droves. They hadn't even turned the camera on yet.

Olivia broke away from the news crew. "Are Maddox's friends still here?" She looked around at the people in the crowd.

I smirked. "No. Why? Did you want to see Flash again?"

She met my eyes. "No."

I nudged her. "Liar."

"Okay, yes. But only because it would look good for him to have his friends here."

"They wouldn't be seen on camera anyway."

I saw Maddox's family off to the side. His mother, sister, and niece all wore smiles, but Foster looked almost sad.

"Excuse me a moment," I said to Olivia.

"Okay."

I walked over to his family. I wasn't sure how they'd respond to me because it was my father's assistant who'd tried to frame Maddox, but they were all smiles as I approached.

"You did it, Addison," Serena said.

I blushed from the praise. "Not really. But I'm super glad that everything turned out okay for Maddox."

Betty took my hand. Her fingers were ice cold, a reminder that she was sick and that she and Maddox didn't have a lot of time to spend with each other. Just another reason I was happy that everything had ended up the way it did.

"We know how hard you fought for him," Betty said.

I looked behind me at Maddox. "He means a lot to me. I wasn't going to let him go without a fight."

She patted my hand as I turned back around to her.

"Hey, Foster, do you mind if I talk to you for a minute?"

His eyes widened in surprise. "Uh…sure."

"I'll bring him right back," I said.

Foster and I walked to the side of the crowd where we wouldn't be overheard.

"Maybe it's time to exonerate your brother for something he didn't do." I nodded toward the camera crew. "Now seems like the perfect opportunity to tell the truth."

"You knew it was me?"

"Yes."

"And you never told anyone?"

"Maddox wouldn't have wanted me to. He loves you very much, you know."

Foster kicked the rocks at his feet. "I know. That's why I feel so bad."

"You know, the statute of limitations on the robbery ran

out years ago. And, while they could go after you for the death of George Fike, the prosecution isn't going to waste its time with that. He wasn't stabbed; he wasn't accidentally shot. He had a heart attack. They wouldn't spend time or taxpayer dollars on a case they'd probably lose."

"I know. It's just...I've worked so hard to build up my reputation and business in this town. I don't want everyone to look at me..."

"Like the way they look at Maddox?"

Guilt washed over Foster's face. "Yes. I sound like a horrible person."

If he was waiting for me to argue, it wasn't going to happen.

"Attention, everyone. We're going live in less than a minute. Please be quiet and don't interrupt the interview," someone on the crew said.

I squeezed Foster's arm. "I know that you know the right thing to do. I'll let you think about it."

I walked away to let him think. I wasn't going to pressure him. He needed to make a decision on his own.

I pushed my way in front of everyone. I wasn't going to miss Maddox being on live TV. He hated it, and I thought it was so cute to see my alpha male be uncomfortable about the whole thing.

The reporter asked him questions about the attempted murder charge, and Maddox handled it well. He said he'd always known justice would prevail and that the truth would come out. She asked if he knew who had committed the crime. Apparently, the news hadn't heard yet. And Maddox said the suspect was only an acquaintance. She moved on and asked him some questions about the Navy. There was only one time the reporter veered off from where he was comfortable, and she reworded her question after he refused to answer.

"You're still young. Is there a reason you retired when you did?"

"I wanted to spend more time with my family," Maddox said. "I hadn't seen them for twelve years. It was time to come home. I wouldn't have been able to get through all this without them."

"Is there anyone else you'd like to thank?" the reporter asked. "Is there a special someone in your life?"

"Now that you mention it." He crooked his finger at me.

I raised my brow. *No way.* I wasn't going over there.

"Olivia? A little help, please?" Maddox said.

Two small hands were suddenly at my back, pushing me toward Maddox. When I was close enough to him, he grabbed my hand and yanked me toward him. He made sure to keep a firm grip around my waist.

I smiled, but inside, I vowed to kill him. My hair was piled on top of my head in a messy bun, I wasn't wearing any makeup, and I was wearing yoga pants and an old flannel shirt tied at the waist. And not in a cute way where my belly button was showing. It was oversize and hung on me. We were supposed to be cleaning. Not be on the news.

"This is my fiancée, Addison."

Fiancée?

The reporter looked at my bare ring finger. "Is this a new thing?"

"Addison and I are high school sweethearts and recently became reacquainted when I came back to town. The engagement is very new."

"And not quite official," I said into the microphone, turning away a little as I felt him let go of me. "He didn't propose to me or anything. It was something we joked about earlier today." I felt like it was my duty to clarify things.

Maddox cleared his throat, and I looked over at him.

He was down on one knee. With a ring box in his hand.

"Addison Graham, will you do me the honor of being my wife?"

I started crying, and Maddox's smile wavered for a split second.

I stared at the ring and almost forgot he was waiting for an answer.

"Yes. Yes. A million times yes."

Maddox's smile turned into a grin, and he stood and opened the box. Inside was a tiny princess cut solitaire diamond on a white gold band.

"I saved all my money the summer before my senior year in high school to buy this. I know it's small, but I want you to have it. I'll buy you something bigger soon."

I started hiccuping because I was crying so hard. "Don't you dare. It's perfect."

Maddox removed the ring from the box and slipped it on my finger. It was a little tight, but right now, it was the best present I'd ever received in my entire life.

I threw my arms around him as I noticed that everyone was clapping for us.

Maddox kissed me and then whispered, "Now, everyone knows that you're mine."

I laughed. "Yeah, they do." I raised my brow. "And you're mine."

He grinned and kissed me again.

52

MADDOX

I turned back to the camera, and Addison rested her head on my chest as the reporter asked a few more questions.

"Addison, you are part of the project that is building a new golf course here; is that correct?"

She lifted her head. She hadn't been prepared to be asked any questions, but like Olivia had said, this was good publicity. "Yes, although things have slowed a bit while Brandon Taylor has been in the hospital. I think they're hoping to have it done by next spring."

"And I heard there was some controversy about some of the homes in the area being torn down to make room for the new construction."

This lady. She had to remind us of the one bad thing in the middle of all this good. This was why I hadn't wanted to do the interview in the first place.

"No houses are being torn down," Addison said. "It is a mobile home park. Each resident owns their own trailer. We just need new land for them to move the homes to." She looked up at me, and I smiled. "We're working on it, but you can understand that, with everything that has happened lately, we've been delayed."

"I might be able to help with that," a feminine voice said in the crowd.

We all looked over to see Claire stepping out from the throng of people with Ben at her side. Her eye was a greenish-yellow color now, but at least it was open, and she could use it. The opposite cheek was also yellowish-green. This was what she looked like after a week. I wanted to find Mickey Williams and kill him.

"Maddox," Ben yelled the minute he saw me.

I picked up the boy as soon as he ran to my arms and smiled. "Hey, buddy. How are you?"

He wrinkled his nose. "I had to stay with some weird people for some days, but now that Mommy's back, I get to go home with her."

The reporter's eyes lit as she realized whom Claire and Ben were. "Claire Williams?" She looked at Ben. "Young man, can you tell me—"

I narrowed my eyes and shook my head at her. She was not traumatizing this boy again.

She cleared her throat. "Can you tell me how you know Maddox?"

"He's friends with Addison, and Addison is friends with Mommy. And, now, Maddox is my friend, too. We played Army together."

"Ben, that was supposed to be our secret."

Ben cupped his mouth and giggled. "Maddox said his Wavy friends wouldn't like him pretending to be an Army guy."

"Navy."

"Huh?"

"My Navy friends."

Ben shrugged and wiggled, so I set him down.

He ran over to his mom and grabbed her hand. "Come on, Mommy. Tell Addison your idea."

She wrung her hands, shying away from the camera, but she still stepped forward. "I would be willing to sell my land if you would take it."

"But what about—" I almost said Mickey.

Thankfully, Claire laughed at my blunder. "It's being taken care of. My lawyer says I will be able to do what I want with the house and land. It's yours."

Addison pulled Claire into a hug. "You're amazing."

Claire's cheeks were now red.

When Addison let her go, I stuck out my hand. "Thank you. My mother, my siblings, and I appreciate it."

She smiled at me. It was timid, but I'd take it. "Thank you. And please tell your friends thank you, too."

"I will."

The reporter looked at me, and I knew the question that I had said absolutely no to was coming.

"This is great news for your community. Do you think, with this recent development along with the charges being dropped, that you've redeemed yourself in the eyes of your town for what happened twelve years ago?"

I clenched my jaw and barely pried it apart to say, "As you remember, the case was dismissed."

"Yes, I'm well aware, but I also know small towns have very long memories."

She was like a pit bull.

I was about to tell her to fuck off on television when I heard my brother's voice.

"Excuse me, I have something to say about that." He stepped next to me.

"What are you doing?"

"It's time, Maddox."

"You don't have to do this," I told him, meaning it.

"Maddox, yes, I do." He took a deep breath and said, "It was me who robbed the gas station twelve years ago."

EPILOGUE

ADDISON

From the doorway of our bedroom, I watched my new husband yank his bow tie off and throw it across the room.

I rushed over and picked it up off the floor. "Hey, we have to turn this in to the tux rental place tomorrow." I set the bow tie on our dresser.

Maddox and I'd bought a house about ten months ago. It was an older home, and Maddox had been busy with remodeling things one room at a time. He'd insisted the bedroom be first. I'd insisted the kitchen be second. That had been a rough few months.

Maddox let his jacket slide down his arms and set it on top of the bow tie. "Sorry, Addy. I've had it with being dressed up." He was struggling to unbutton the shirt. His fingers were too big.

I pushed his hands aside. "Let me." I began unbuttoning him myself. "So, you don't like being dressed up, but did you have fun?"

"Yes." He smiled wickedly at me. "But I'm going to have

more fun now." He reached behind me and began unzipping my dress. His brows furrowed when it didn't fall off me right away.

I laughed and paused my unbuttoning to pull the tulle from underneath. My dress immediately fell to the floor.

"What the hell is that?"

"Something to make my dress look fuller without adding more fabric."

He looked at me like I was crazy. "This is why the bride and groom can't see each other before the ceremony."

"You're probably right." I finished taking the buttons apart on his shirt and pushed it off his shoulders. "Maddox Wolfe. Navy SEAL, sheriff, husband." *Alpha male,* I added to myself.

He smiled. "That's me."

After Simon had been charged with Brandon's attempted murder, getting thirty years in prison, Detective Porter had begun to look more into Sheriff Whitlock's conduct. Detective Porter thought there might be enough to press charges. However, the consensus in town was that, if Sheriff Whitlock stepped down and avoided future law enforcement positions, he wouldn't be charged.

With the position open, I encouraged Maddox to run. I knew it was very different from being in the Navy, but I thought he could do some good for our little town and our county. Plus, it would give him a sense of accomplishment. He'd been cleaning up the department the last few months. He complained sometimes, but I thought he secretly liked it.

It had taken the town a little while to get over the scandal that Foster had committed the crime that everyone had blamed Maddox for, but they'd learned to forgive Foster. Most of them anyway. And those same people had opened their minds to Maddox being a good guy. So much that he had been voted into office.

Brandon had made a full recovery and finished the golf course as the lead on the project. It made life easier that the golf course was constructed, and Maddox's mom had relocated to the new trailer park. Claire had taken the money and bought herself and Ben a nicer house in town and was now working at the country club. In the end, everything had worked out.

Maddox ran his thumb down my cheek. "Addison Wolfe. Attorney-at-law and wife."

"What would you think if we added one more title to our names?"

He raised an eyebrow. "Oh, and what would that be?"

I touched my finger to my chest. "Mommy." Then, I touched his. "And Daddy."

Maddox blinked a few times before hauling me into his arms and lifting my feet off the floor. "When did you find out?" he asked, setting me back down and staring at my belly with wide eyes.

"This morning. I was feeling off the last week or so, and I thought I'd better check before I drank champagne today."

He grinned. "So, that's what was with the sparkling cider at the last minute. Why didn't you tell me this morning?"

"I wanted it to be your special wedding present from me when we got home."

"Oh, Addy, it's special all right." He kissed me and slowly took off the rest of my clothes. "I need to be inside you right now."

I reached for his pants and unzipped them. "I completely understand."

"Get on the bed, wife."

I grinned and walked backward to the bed. I lay down and spread my legs for him.

Maddox groaned. "When can we tell people?"

"In about five to six weeks, I'm guessing. We'll find out when I go to the doctor. Why do you ask?"

"Because I can't wait to tell the world another way that I've marked you as mine."

I laughed and held out my arms. "Take me, Maddox. Right now, I need you to show *me* that I belong to you."

TAKE ME IN THE DARK EXCERPT

OLIVIA

As I drove into Brook Creek, I noted once again how different it was from Des Moines. I hadn't been to the small town since Addison and Maddox got married. Whenever I got together with the two of them, they came to Des Moines. I thought I had forgotten just how little their town was. It felt safer, and right now, I could use safer. My last case had taken a toll on me.

When I had started my own firm, I'd had to be there practically all the time. But we were big enough now, with enough associates and a couple of unnamed partners, that I could take a few days off. It was going to be tough for me not to call in every hour while I was gone though. Even after all I'd been through, I would never abandon my work.

Putting all that out of my mind, I walked into Addison's office, grateful for the air-conditioning. Summers were hot in Iowa.

"Hello," Addison's assistant greeted me.

I had never met her before. Maddox's niece used to work

for Addison, but now that she was close to graduating, working for Addison had gotten to be too much for Serena.

"How can I help you?"

"I'm Olivia. Addison is expecting me."

"Come back here," Addison yelled from her private office.

I chuckled. "Thanks," I told the assistant and walked back.

Addison stood from behind her desk and came around to give me a hug. "I'm so glad you came."

When we separated, I looked her up and down. "Did you doubt that I would?"

Her brown eyes lit up with a smile and a tad of guilt. "I thought maybe you were going to change your mind."

I laughed. "I did think about it once or twice, but I'm here."

"And I'm glad you are." She looked at her desk. "Do you mind if I finish up this one thing, and then I'll take you upstairs to the apartment?"

"Sure. I'll check my email while I wait."

Addison pointed to the open chairs while she took her seat back at her desk. "Sit wherever."

I sat off to the right in the corner chair to give Addison space to work and pulled out my phone.

There was a message from my assistant, Derek.

Derek: Another letter came.

I took in a deep breath, counted to five, and exhaled.

Me: What does it say?

Derek: Same as all the others.

Me: Throw it away.

Derek: Are you sure, Little Miss Don't Ever Get Rid of Evidence?

Me: I'm sure.

Derek: Okay. You're the boss.

Me: Call me if anything else comes up.

I closed the Messages app and opened my email. I didn't want to think about Derek's texts. I had wrongly assumed that when my last case was over, the troubles that went with it would also end.

But I wasn't going to focus on that right now. I was on vacation. That stuff could wait until I got back to work.

I hoped anyway.

Turning my thoughts to something I could control, I started reading my email. I was a few in when I heard the front door open.

"Addison busy?" It was Maddox's voice.

I grinned. Even if Maddox was not the type of guy I would ever date, I really liked him and thought of him as a friend and not just the husband of a friend.

But I lost my smile when he walked in and I saw he wasn't alone.

His friend Tommy—aka Flash—was with him, and I was immediately transported back to the first time I had met him back when I was defending Maddox for assault and attempted murder.

• • •

Addison and I were in her office. Addison was behind her desk, and I was sitting in front of her with my feet up on her desk while I watched the news on my laptop. The night before, Maddox and his two friends, Thomas Morelli and Evan Malone, had rescued a mom and son from her ex-husband, who had come back to town and attacked her.

Addison and I were discussing Maddox's case and this new development when the front door opened. Addison looked up and watched through the doorway. I went back to my computer, half-listening to the conversation in the other room.

"Hey, Serena," Maddox said.

"Hey, Uncle Maddox."

"Guys, this is my niece, Serena."

"Hi," she said.

"Serena, this is Tommy, and this is Evan. I used to work with them."

"Nice to meet you," one of them said.

"The rules that apply to Addison also apply to her. Hands off." That was Maddox.

I made a noise, and Addison looked over at me.

"Please tell me I'm not representing some caveman," I said in a low voice.

Addison laughed. "Don't knock it till you try it," she whispered back. "Maddox would never boss me around…except in the bedroom." She wiggled her eyebrows. "There's something hot about being dragged off to the cave by your hair and being taken from behind."

I could feel my eyes widen, and I was sure I was looking at her like she was crazy. "No, thank you. I'll stick to nice, respectable men who treat me like a lady."

"Your orgasms must suck," a deep voice said from behind me, "and be super boring."

I jumped in my seat, and Addison almost spit out the coffee she had just taken a sip of.

I dropped my feet, turned around in my chair, and glared at the man who'd had the balls to say something like that to me. He didn't even know me.

I had to concentrate on keeping the look on my face and not showing any surprise when I saw the person who had insulted me. He was huge. Taller than an already-tall Maddox and full of muscle with dark brown hair and deep brown eyes.

I swallowed hard but retained my composure.

Piecing together the picture from the news and the info Addison had told me, I knew this guy must be Tommy.

What kind of grown man goes by Tommy?

Unfazed by my anger, he shrugged at me. "If you even have any at all. Excuse me, miss. I'd like to make you come now,*" he said in a voice slightly higher than his own. "*Okay, but be careful. I can't ruin my hair or my makeup,*" Tommy said, pretending to be me.*

If I were a cartoon, smoke would be coming out of my nostrils. "You don't even know me."

Tommy laughed. "I've met your kind before. Big and bad to the world, but behind closed doors, you need your ass slapped and your pussy pounded."

I gasped. This guy had some nerve.

"Flash," Maddox said, coming into the room, "leave my lawyer alone. I want her to defend me, not run away, cursing my name because of my friends." He stepped around his friend. "Please don't throw my trial because of one asshole."

Poor Maddox. He needed to invest in finding new friends.

I patted his hand. "Don't worry. I've dealt with worse men than him before." I looked at said asshole. "Nice name," I said sarcastically.

He snickered. "It's a nickname, sweetheart." He raised his eyebrows. "You can ask Addison about it later."

I threw my hair over my shoulder. "I don't think so."

Tommy shrugged. "Like I said, boring." He laid his head on his shoulder and pretended to snore.

Maddox socked him in the gut. "Knock it off, asswipe."

Then, he walked over to Addison's chair and lifted her out of her seat. She squealed.

He sat down in her chair and settled her on his lap. "So, what do you want to go over today?" Maddox asked and nuzzled Addison's neck.

I had to turn my eyes away as the uncomfortable feeling of jealousy filled my gut.

Thankfully, another man, who had to be Evan, walked into the office, reminding me to answer Maddox's question.

"Well, first, congratulations are in order for what happened early this morning. This will look very good to any potential jury," I said.

Tommy scowled. "Mad Dog didn't do it for the publicity. We did it because someone was in trouble."

I sighed. "I know that. But it helps our case nonetheless."

It wasn't that I didn't feel bad for the victim—because I did. A lot. It was that I was looking at the big picture. And that meant getting Maddox cleared of all charges or found not guilty in a court of law.

"She's kind of right," Evan said. "Everyone was waiting to shake Mad Dog's hand when we went to get breakfast this morning. Ours, too. But they were looking at Mad Dog like he was a hero."

Maddox scowled. "Everyone likes me now, I guess." He said something else that only Addison could hear.

She kissed him on the cheek. "You don't need them."

I went over a few more things with Maddox, and then the guys took off.

Addison went through some of her paperwork while I did some work on my computer. Unfortunately, I couldn't stop thinking about

Tommy telling me to ask Addison about his nickname. I really didn't want to know. But I did.

Damn my curiosity.

"Ask me," Addison said, not looking up from her desk.

"What?" I didn't think I had been that obvious.

She lifted her head. "I know you want to know, Olivia. Ask me."

I rolled my eyes. "How did Flash get his nickname? And what is his real name? I wasn't actually introduced." I did already know, but I didn't want to admit that I had paid attention to who he was.

"His name is Tommy. And he got the nickname because he said the ladies are gone in a flash when they go out to the bar."

"I can see why." I frowned. "He made it sound like his nickname was a good thing."

"Well, apparently, the women avoid him because they're afraid of his size."

"He is a big guy. But I didn't get the impression he'd hurt anyone."

Addison laughed. "No, not his body size. The size of his dick."

My cheeks heated.

Addison and I had met in college, but we had been more classroom friends. We hadn't hung out with the same people. None of my friends would ever say something so blunt out loud. Not that they didn't talk about sex. They just hinted about those things more and used code words.

"Oh," I said as I fingered the corner of my laptop. "That never occurred to me."

Addison chuckled. "Maybe Tommy is right, and you've been with the wrong guys. You haven't had sex until you've had sex with someone with a big cock."

My eyes widened. "Does Maddox..." The question slipped out before I could stop it.

"Hell yeah. Why do you think I can't keep my hands off him? It's big, and he knows what to do with it."

"I've never had that." Again, my mouth was speaking before my brain could stop it.

Addison grinned. "I'm sure Flash would be more than happy to show you."

I stiffened my spine. "No, thank you."

But deep inside my mind—way in the back, where no one was ever allowed—I imagined what it would be like to have sex with him. I shut that down after two seconds. Now was not the time to think about sex.

Addison gave me a once-over. "You're probably right. He might break you in two."

I shuddered at the memory. Addison had been right. I didn't know if someone my size could even handle someone as big as Tommy.

And why am I even thinking about this?

Tommy and I weren't going to sleep together.

"Ooh la la," Addison said. "Two sexy, sweaty men, walking down the street." It was clear by the clothes—or lack thereof since Tommy had opted to take his shirt off and tuck it into his shorts—and sweat that Maddox and Tommy had been doing some sort of workout, and she was right. One blond and one brunette. They looked pretty sexy together. "Did you two have to fight off all the women with a stick?"

Maddox held up his left hand and wiggled his ring finger. "They know I'm taken and I'd never stray."

"Aw," Addison said.

"Yeah, aw. But stop ogling my friend," Maddox joked.

"I'm married, not blind, Maddox," she teased back with an eyebrow wiggle.

Tommy pretended to smooth down his nonexistent shirt. I swallowed. Even from my seat off to the side, I could see he had a very nice torso with perfectly sculpted muscles.

And I didn't like it.

"Thanks for noticing, Addison. Don't worry, Mad; I'll keep your woman away from me."

"At least someone has my back," Maddox muttered.

Addison rolled her eyes and pointed to me.

Both men turned, and Maddox grinned. "Hey, Olivia. I didn't see you there."

I stood and gave him a hug. "Hey, Maddox."

After I stepped back, he pointed to Tommy. "You remember my friend Tommy, right? You met him the first time you came to Brook Creek, and he was also a guest at our wedding."

I shot Addison a quick look for not telling me that Tommy would be here. Then, I furrowed my brow as if I were confused and shook my head. "Sorry. Doesn't ring a bell."

ACKNOWLEDGMENTS

We'd like to thank our editor, Jovana Shirley, our beta readers, our ARC readers, and the bloggers who share our books. We couldn't do this without you!

Thanks to our families, and thanks to all our author friends who share our posts and books. Your support means everything!

ABOUT THE AUTHOR

R.L. Kenderson is two best friends writing under one name.

Renae has always loved reading, and in third grade, she wrote her first poem where she learned she might have a knack for this writing thing. Lara remembers sneaking her grandmother's Harlequin novels when she was probably too young to be reading them, and since then, she knew she wanted to write her own.

When they met in college, they bonded over their love of reading and the TV show *Charmed*. What really spiced up their friendship was when Lara introduced Renae to romance novels. When they discovered their first vampire romance, they knew there would always be a special place in their hearts for paranormal romance. After being unable to find certain storylines and characteristics they wanted to read about in the hundreds of books they consumed, they decided to write their own.

One lives in the Minneapolis-St. Paul area and the other in the Kansas City area where they both work in the medical field during the day and a sexy author by night. They communicate through phone, email, and whole lot of messaging.

You can find them at http://www.rlkenderson.com, Facebook, Instagram, TikTok, and Goodreads. Join their reader group! Or you can email them at rlkenderson@rlkenderson

.com, or sign up for their newsletter. They always love hearing from their readers.

www.ingramcontent.com/pod-product-compliance
Lightning Source LLC
Chambersburg PA
CBHW070655180626
46817CB00006B/2383

9781950918188